good deed rain

He wondered what Philip Marlowe would do...stuck behind a painted line in an alley full of rain...a lost book of Japanese poetry...and a fifty year old spoon in his coat pocket.

Books by Allen Frost

ISLAND AIR

Island Air © 2019
Allen Frost, Good Deed Rain
Bellingham, Washington
ISBN 978-1-64633-561-9

Writing: Allen Frost
Cover Photo: Joel Aparicio
Cover Production: Jen Armitage
Leaves: Allen Frost
Apple: TFK!

For Aaron

Credits:
The Expressman and the Detective, Allan Pinkerton, W.B. Keen, Cooke & Col, 1874.
The Earth We Live On, Frederick Warne and Co., London, 1875.
Martians Go Home, Fredric Brown, E.P. Dutton & Co., Inc. New York, 1955.
Technicians of the Sacred: A Range of Poetries from Africa, America, Asia & Oceania, collected and edited by Jerome Rothenberg, Doubleday & Co. Inc., NY, 1968.
Movies: *Idiot's Delight* (1939) *The Lady Eve* (1941).

Cool air
wherever you are
Mount Fuji

—Issa

ISLAND AIR

ALLEN FROST

Good Deed Rain ◊ Bellingham, Washington ◊ 2019

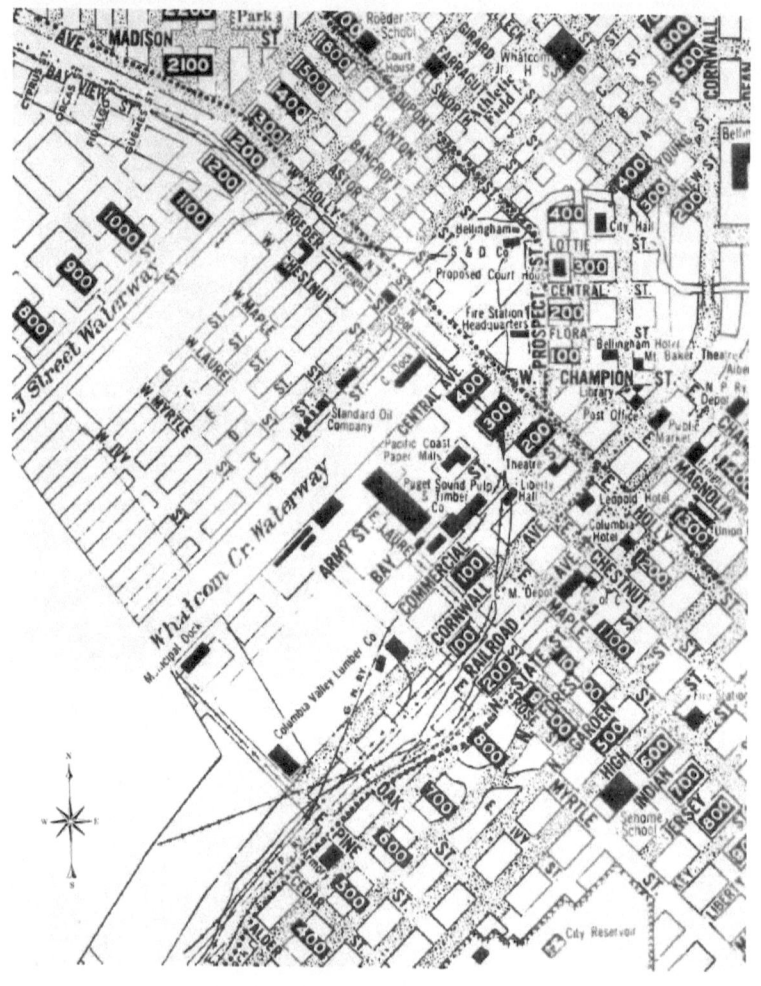

CONTENTS

MAT AND MILLIES GOOD EATS CAFE

March 4, 1948

RICE TOMATO SOUP

POTATO   VEGETABLE   DESSERT
        45¢   45¢
Vegetable Plate
Hot Beef Sandwich
Black Cod with French Fried Potatoes
Weiners and Sauerkraut

        50¢   50¢
Braized Sirloin Tips
Grilled Spring Salmon
Roast Sirloin of Beef
Hamburger Steak with Brown Gravy
Home Made Sausage
Fried Fillet of Sole
Little Pig Sausages with Brown Gravy
Baked Heart with Dressing

        Milk 5¢ Extra with all Meals
        * * * * * * * * * * *

60¢ Cube Steak with French Fried Potatoes
60¢ Fried Fresh Oysters
75¢ Rib Steak with French Fried Potatoes
65¢ Pork Chops with French Fried Potatoes

Coffee, or Buttermilk with all meals

Tea or Cocoa 10¢   All Pies 10¢ per cut

        * * *

CHAPTER ONE

Morning, 1992

I tried my best to hold back summer from leaving but in the end I couldn't. It slipped away. Vatican Jones let that thought rise and fall. The nights are getting colder, the gray clouds will come down from Canada and rain and wind are waiting just offshore, just out of sight behind the islands.

That's okay, he thought, It happens every year, I have learned what to do. On the corner of Champion and Holly, The Old Crown café sits and steams like a warm kettle in the early morning.

"More coffee, VJ?" the waitress asked.

"Oh yes. Yes please." He pushed the cup her way and she refilled it. Not a drop was lost. The coffee seemed to pour directly from her arm, swirled from the glass Silex bulb like a Martian flower. "Another summer is gone," he said.

She agreed and gave the gray window a look with him. "It was nice though." She patted his shoulder, "And it always comes back."

"That's right." He wrapped his fingers around the cup. Across the road, the streetlights were still on from last night. They stood on the slanting hillside waiting for the sun to take over. That's when the moths were going home to roost, to hang up their wings under eaves. After years of haiku, that's the way Vatican thought.

Vatican Jones, or more simply VJ also had another alias, the one his mother gave him when he was born in August, 1945. He was named for that auspicious day—Victory Japan—when the war was finally over. But like Shakespeare said, what's in a name anyway? For a while he preferred Vatican Jones—he went through many years with that name. He still thought of himself that way sometimes. Anytime he was confronted with a mystery. But as he grew older and seemed to understand more, he eventually arrived at a simple name: VJ. Still, it depended on who he was talking to. Old friends only knew him as Vatican.

He took a sip of coffee.

Past the streetlamps, the paper factory, the docks and the bay, gray as laid out slate, a crab boat bounced along the water towards the islands.

"Here you are," the waitress said as she returned and clicked a plate before him.

"Oh, thank you." An egg sandwich. His usual. He never could bring himself to go beyond those shores, even though the menu had other meals to choose from. They even had Baked Heart. He always checked to make sure it was still there. He wondered if they kept one frozen for a special occasion.

Before he put the muffin lid on his sandwich, he added some pepper, some hot sauce and pulled the plate closer. A green sprig of parsley, small as a bonsai tree, grew next to the food. It made him wonder if Basho made this meal.

When he looked outside again, the streetlights were dimmed. They must have felt the sun. The new day had begun.

A guitar strummed.

Like an ingredient dropped into soup, the instrument mixed with the rest of the sound in the big wooden room.

VJ didn't have to turn around to know who was playing "The Bells of Rhymney" behind him. It was just as clear as Ryokan.

The Old Crown had its regulars—VJ supposed he could be counted as one of them—but in a group of their own were the musicians. The café had a policy of giving any player of instrument a free meal for an hour's worth of music.

"And who killed the miner? Say the grim bells of Lind."

Another sip of coffee and it was nearly time to set sail. Outside wasn't just a picture or a movie screen—it was a world waiting for him to join in.

He stood up and got some money from his book. He left some dollars on the tabletop beside his empty cup and turned around.

Nickels hung onto the guitar as if his life depended on it, in a flooded mine disaster a hundred feet below the ground. It was best not to disturb him when he was in the throws. As VJ walked past, he tossed a dollar in the cardboard shoebox.

The menu was also written in chalk on the wall above the register. He noticed the Baked Heart again.

"Bye VJ," his waitress called.

He waved the book he carried. *The Year of My Life*, by the poet Issa. The cover looked like the backlot behind the building he lived in. Weeds overgrowing the world. A rained on patch of bamboo, grass and blackberry vines. It was easy to feel a connection to those Japanese haiku poets. This could almost be Japan, this factory town set by the bay with the green islands and fog, like its own landscape running across three folding screens.

Someone held the door open and he nodded and walked into the breeze again. He could smell the salt on the air.

Nickels faded when the door shut and after a few steps more the song was gone. There were other sounds: cars, gulls, the factory breathing loud as a hungry dragon.

He followed Holly, crossing Champion, hopped up the curb on the other side. He walked beside a parking lot slanting with a few cars. Across the tar was the creek. Holly Street crept over it on the posts of old cedar poles and clacking wooden bridge slats.

Sinbad's Treasure was on the other side of the street. VJ was easily tempted by the huge antique store. Last time he went in, he got lost for a couple hours and finally came out with an antique dog whistle. It must have been silver at one time, before it got so gray. He supposed if he ever dared to blow it, it would attract dog ghosts. That was something that might be useful someday.

Sinbad's was also where he bought the little record of "Soldier Boy" by the Shirelles. That was their song.

Where the sidewalk leveled out, he could have followed a path to his right, towards the salmon hatchery, the creek and the ruins of the old windmill. It had been years since he went that way, not since the days when "Soldier Boy" used to play from the rooftop.

He crossed Holly when the coast was clear. It could be a busy street sometimes. Just down from Sinbad's, on the corner, another antique building grew. That's where he lived.

The Sea of Tranquility had tall windows that faced the street. You could look in through the venetian blinds and see the big room inside. Like the photo of an old factory floor tinted with the pale color light of our modern day. A seaplane from 1917 was being slowly assembled by hand. All the parts of it filled the room. The wings were leaned against the wall, the hull gleamed with varnish. It looked like all it needed was another day to be fit together so it could fly.

VJ noticed the glow in the window and was glad. That meant Martin was probably there.

Around the other side of the building, in the driveway to the backlot, a stair led up from the dirt to a door. VJ caught himself humming Nickel's song. A crow above him scratched as it walked along the gutter. The factory was making clouds, sending them out across the bay. Some of them would curl around the peaks of the fir covered islands, others would keep drifting until they found somewhere else.

As he rounded the wooden siding, VJ had to stop. The door was only another ten feet away. There was just enough room in the alley between The Sea of Tranquility and the Sunshine Dairy office to bring a milk truck through, to park on the mud and gravel behind Sinbad's. The railroad tracks went along the water. The trains would rumble by, shaking the blackberry piles and rattling the puddles spread across the muddy lot.

As if none of this existed at all—as if it was still Douglas fir and ground cover—on the memory of a path that ran through here like a stream, a deer stood in front of him.

CHAPTER TWO

Making Haiku

Off to the side in the room with the airplane, near the tracks of the rolling door, was a smaller workplace with its own wooden creation.

Any resemblance to a boat was not intentional. VJ was following strict guidelines for his construction, guidelines just as detailed as those for building that Curtis Seagull biplane that filled the rest of the room.

VJ's directions were simpler, that's all. Written on a scrap of paper taped to the wall were three simple lines: 5 x 7 x 5. Haiku, translated into height, width, depth.

Made out of pine and spruce scrap wood, rigging wire and anything else the plane didn't need, this box-like work of carpentry was his haiku. It even said so, painted in black letters high up on the stern: Haiku.

A ladder leaned against the tall hull. It was hard to tell how far the boat would settle in the water. It was possible it wouldn't float at all. Maybe it would be a submarine.

Across the room, the alley door opened wide and shut. Martin carried a tall cup of coffee and he called out, "Hey Vatican! You here?" He took a sip while he listened.

Hidden inside the boat, the sound of a rocking chair stopped and VJ's voice answered like a bell.

Martin laughed. The whole big room seemed to know he was back and welcomed him, creaking floorboards around his feet like a cat rubbing his legs as he walked. He passed all the parts of his airplane flocked along tabletops. A V-8 engine block was cradled in the air. He took a deep breath of that wood and oil and declared, "Vatican Jones in his coffin!" Martin stopped beside Haiku and rested a hand on the rim. Inside that 5 x 7 x 5 he could see his old friend resting in a rocking chair, a book perched on his knee. "Hard at work?"

VJ lay a hand on the wall beside him. "I was thinking of putting a window here. Maybe one on the other side too."

Martin nodded. He set his coffee cup where his hand had been and reached into the pocket of his black wool coat. He held a rolled copy of *The Wise Penny*. Its pages snapped and crackled as they turned.

VJ could hear the slow puffing approach of Martin's 14 year old dog, Gertrude. She followed in his tracks like a steam-engine dog. Her breathing sawed.

"Here you go," Martin said and passed the newspaper into the boat.

The print was small. Fortunately a thick lead pencil had drawn a loop around the notice. VJ didn't have his glasses. He didn't like to admit he needed them. "Ahah!" he said as he held the page close and read, "Portholes for sale!"

Martin took a sip of coffee. "I must have known what you were thinking."

"Yes. This is perfect." How funny that his thoughts had been broadcast, received, printed and carried back to him on paper. "Pacific Supply is just down the street." VJ clambered out of Haiku.

Gertrude watched him appear out of nowhere. She caught her breath for a moment, ears raised. She was nearly deaf and all she really saw was a blurry world. She stood next to the smell of Martin's black coat.

When VJ left the last ladder step, he patted the

spot where a porthole should go. "A couple windows and then I think she's done." He pictured floating in Haiku, halfway to the nearest island. A sunny blue October day on the water. He wouldn't want to lean over the edge, the boat might be easy to tip. When Martin first saw the plans he said, "That's not a boat, that's a piano crate!" VJ took that as a compliment. It made him think of Beethoven, Chopin, Debussy, playing in the middle of the bay. He was pleased with the idea of portholes, he could stay centered in the boat, sitting in his rocking chair and see out either side. "Do you want to take a look at them with me?" He gave Gertrude's head a scratch. She was back to sawing a circle in the air.

"I think we better stay. Gert's a little overheated."

"Okay. Is it raining?"

"Not yet." The way Martin stared at the boat, you could tell there was something he wanted to say—it was about as opposite as possible from the sculpted ornate flying machine it shared the room with. VJ knew it wasn't how Martin would make a boat, but that was okay—that's what made it Haiku.

It wasn't raining yet, but it was on the way. It was broadcast in the air. If you were a flower or a frog, you'd be waiting with open arms.

VJ shut the door behind him and returned to the sidewalk. The traffic seemed to have picked up along Holly Street. He didn't know how long he had been reading in Haiku. Even if it never floated, it was nice to sit in. You could stare at all the twigs and branches and whorls in the wood or you could close your eyes. Sometimes a couple hours slipped away.

Across the street, above the trees and rooftops, watched the City Hall steeple. They didn't give the time away for free—the clock on it was frozen at 7. The pigeons creaked around the eaves on a worn down ledge. It was sort of a joke in town—if someone asked you for the time, you would always say 7 o'clock.

There was something else unusual about that tall red tower with 1896 painted on its bricks. One morning at The Old Crown, someone told VJ about the ghost. That news wasn't too surprising—City Hall looked like a ghost itself, a gothic pointed Victorian apparition time traveling through to 1992. Somewhere during that flight into the future, a ghost got caught in the whirling gears. It held on to the bannister and would creak up and down the stairway from the basement to the attic, from dusk to dawn.

The tower ducked behind the yellow leaves of a tree and VJ returned his vision to the sidewalk in front of him. A homeless man with a red white and blue top hat pushed a bicycle across the grass. Pacific Supply wasn't far from Lighthouse mission.

If a cartographer followed VJ from day to day it would soon be clear he had narrowed down the world to a pretty small map with a few well-worn paths. He wasn't much unlike a garden snail. What more did he need than some flowers and a bucket's worth of dew?

That's when he saw 99. She was headed his way, going up the hill towards the center of town. He usually saw her in front of the record store or on the corner by the photocopy shop. He had to admire 99's fashion style. Overnight, she went from wearing baggy pink sweatpants and parka, looking desperate as a tornado victim on TV, to what used to be called Roller Derby Queen. Black tights under cutoff jeans and black leather jacket. That look also happened to be the new dress code of Seattle grunge. Some of the young had that uniform. Today she was wearing a long shirt that said Nirvana. He always said hello. She always turned to him as if they had never met and started her spiel. "Everything in the store is 99 cents. Lots and lots of great deals." Then, it never failed, she leaned in close to add conspiratorially as she handed him a photocopied flyer, "No expiration date."

He waved to 99 as she neared and she reached into her handbag and he knew here we go again.

She held a lime green flyer in her hand.

He knew he had about three seconds.

She offered him the piece of paper. "Everything in the store is 99 cents. We have lots of good deals today."

He was close enough she could whisper loudly, "No expiration date," as she put the flyer in his hand.

"Thanks."

"You know how to find The 99 Cent Store?"

"Sure," VJ said. "But I have to go to a different store."

"What for? We have everything you need—food, clothes, household goods—all for less than a dollar."

"That's true," he nodded. "Maybe I'll stop by later."

"You should!"

"Okay. Thank you for this." He waved the flyer. She wore bright yellow hi-top sneakers with pink laces. How did he miss that detail before?

"Have a good day."

"You too. Goodbye." He almost said, "Goodbye, 99." Even though he saw her every day, he didn't know her actual name. But he doubted she was named for a discount store. Maybe she would remember him if he asked.

Of course he had been in The 99 Cent Store

before. There were rows of plastic. From the moment you opened the door you were lost in it. And she was right: they had cheap versions of almost anything you could want, but he doubted they had portholes.

He took a deep breath and closed his eyes. There were days it smelled like the ocean had crawled into the air. You never knew when it would happen, the conditions had to be just right for that ghostly tide to leave the shallows, climb the breakwater and cross the railroad tracks sweeping into town. For a while you could feel that pull, ebb and flow, that moves the fish around. VJ liked to let go and swim with the air wherever it flowed. Maybe he wouldn't make it to Pacific Supply, maybe he would wash up somewhere far away. Then it might take him all day to get back to The Sea of Tranquility. When the sun went down, he slept in Haiku.

A Handbook for

AIR RAID
WARDENS

United States
OFFICE OF CIVILIAN DEFENSE
Washington, D. C.

CHAPTER THREE

Soldier Boy

On the same street, 50 years ago, clouds. Did they ever change? Were they the same ones reappearing over islands? Who knew, who kept track? Another morning began. The factory was already smoking. A young woman walked on Holly Street with a book in her hand. She kept an eye on the sky, every cloud could be hiding something she needed to see. She wore a brown wool uniform, a silver whistle and binoculars around her neck. If any Japanese plane happened to fly by, she was ready. But she should have been watching the sea.

Chances are Anita Jones would not have seen the periscope, no bigger than a drainpipe, leading a leaky trail of bubbles towards an unused portion of loading dock. It was still early, there was fog on the water, geese heading south called down from a V in the sky.

Anita turned her binoculars towards them and fell in with their flight. There were no propellers on their wings. She put the book over her mouth and yawned, bringing the binoculars down. The geese turned back into dots lost in the sky. After half a year of watching birds, she almost wished they were Japanese. What was taking them so long?

Wasn't it just like waiting for a boy? How many times had she told her mother, "I'll never find someone, nobody likes me." Every night she sat on the couch in the parlor and listened to the radio alone. Then she would leave for the observation post, a henhouse by the creek, to watch for planes that weren't there.

A loud trolley rattled past on the street, its metal

wheels screeching and she turned her attention from its foggy windows.

A cobbled alley, an oil drum, a broken pallet. Beside a black puddle lay a dead bird. With a cry, she flew to it. Anyone who knew Anita knew that was the first thing she would do.

It was a little sparrow. The cold night had been too much for it. On its back, feet curled up, there was white frost in its feathers.

"Oh no..." she said as she kneeled beside it. She slipped her *Handbook for Air Raid Wardens* into her purse and searched for her handkerchief.

Another trolley clattered, going uphill. The alley echoed with the sound.

Anita carefully wrapped the bird in a square of embroidered silk, soft as a folded parachute. She stood and wondered what to do. If she was at home, she would bury the bird in the garden. An alley wasn't a good cemetery. A volunteer in the Ground Observer Corp had to know the city though—this was her district—and sure as the map memorized in her head, the alley led out to City Hall where there were trees on the slope.

Halfway down the alley, she stopped at The Old Sea Gull Coffee House. This was her morning ritual where she could have breakfast for a Mercury dime, back when Lady Liberty was on the coin.

The heat of a woodstove warmed the room. She had a favorite table seat by the window. The cook caught her eye and waved a spatula as she approached the counter.

Mr. Vermeulen saluted her. After all these mornings the gesture had taken on a seriousness. "We saved your table, Warden."

"Thank you," she said, "but I can't have breakfast quite yet. I was wondering, can I borrow a spoon?"

"A spoon? What kind of a spoon you want, dear? I'll give you the best spoon in the house."

She smiled, "That's okay. Just a regular soup spoon will do fine."

Mr. Vermeulen reached under the counter and with a silvery rustle took one from a nest of others. He polished it on his apron and presented it to her. "You want some soup to go with that spoon?"

"No thank you, Mr. Vermeulen." She didn't want to tell him she was going to use it to bury a bird—she kept that wrapped silk package behind her back. "I'll return soon."

He gave her another salute. He was getting good at that. Everyone was.

It wasn't easy to leave the warmth and smell of The Old Sea Gull. Her spot by the window waved goodbye. She slipped out the door.

An airplane droned above the alley, out of sight behind the brick walls and chimneys, but Anita didn't seem to notice. She was remembering last night's newsreel. An airplane spiraled out of the sky on fire. Black smoke poured off the wings. When it hit the ground, people in the theatre cheered and applauded. One less enemy.

Was there such a thing?

What about that pilot's family? How would they feel? They just lost their son. Imagine the circle that spread from there. She closed her eyes and waited for the comedy feature to start.

A crow flew from her as she left the alley and crossed the street. The black wings were headed to the same place as her. As she left the cement, her shoes and socks were brushed with dew.

The grass was left to get tall, low trees and blackberry grew wild. Sometimes deer would hide in pockets just below City Hall. It was the perfect place to bury her little dead pilot.

Other birds might have known what she was doing, digging the damp ground underneath a tree. Chickadees whispered above her in the branches. Every hop of those tiny feet sent a raindrop her way.

This time of year it wasn't easy to find a flower. There were some dry thistles and some summer burnt remains of petals on bushes. She picked whatever was left, enough to cover her hand, and spilled them on the bird's grave.

She remembered that act clearly, even after 50 years. She could still see the dark petals like the leaves in an empty teacup. A fortune teller would have read them and said, "Your life is about to change." It did too—that was the moment—as she stood contemplating that bird's resting place—her prayer was answered. Someone noticed her.

A yellow leaf shook off a tree. It was quiet enough to hear a flock of snow geese overhead. She turned and saw a man hiding in the October leaves.

He looked like someone waiting for a train. He wore a simple brimmed hat, a rumpled brown suit, and he held a heavy handbag in each hand. No, that wasn't quite right, they weren't bags. They were made of metal. He stood still behind the rhododendron until he was sure she had seen him. When there was no mistaking the way she stared at him, he started out of the leaves.

"Hello," she said.

He gave her a quick nod with a sort of half bow.

No, those weren't suitcases he was carrying, she saw they were two film reel canisters. Some nights at the theatre she saw the projectionist wheezing those by the handles up the stairs to the booth. How long had he been hiding there watching her, holding the weight of a movie world?

Another odd thing about him: he was wearing sunglasses like pictures of those stars in Hollywood. Could he actually be some famous director or movie producer scouting their little town?

She nervously explained, "I was burying a dead bird," and she pointed at the ground near her feet. "My name is Anita."

He set his luggage down and reached into his coat pocket lining, removing a pack of cards. He chose one from the top of the stack and held it out for her.

"I am Umi," she read the fine lettering aloud, "I do not speak."

He nodded, touched his lips and returned the card to the deck.

She carried a deck like that too. It was part of her job as volunteer Air Raid Warden. She had cards she would study that were black pictures of every airplane in the Imperial Japanese Army Air Service. She even memorized the silhouettes of ships and submarines. She knew every war machine. But it didn't occur to her until later that he came from one of them.

"Nice to meet you, Mr. Umi." There was something different about him alright. She figured he was from the circus. Every summer a circus would arrive in town and you would see all kinds of amazing people. And animals would march through town from the station to the field out on Iowa Street. This summer they even lost an elephant. It hid in the creek like a Tarzan movie. Maybe he had also lost his way.

Whoever he was, there was something a little strange about standing in the trees below City Hall on a foggy morning. Her handbook warned her to be vigilant. The words on page 7 spoke to her like a newsreel: "As an Air Raid Warden, you have a unique position in American community life. You must know your people well. To them, you are the embodiment of all Civilian Defense."

She pointed at the film canisters and asked, "Are you bringing those to the theatre?" Was this how they delivered movies during wartime, under the cover of leaves?

He flipped through his cards. He had a lot of answers prepared. When he found the one he wanted, he showed it to her.

"I must go to my ship," she read.

A loud hiss from the factory made him jump and he quickly replaced the card with the others.

"Oh! You're a sailor?"

He nodded. He picked up the metal canisters and she found herself swept along with him.

She could have gone home or back to the coffee house to return their spoon. That would have meant the same old story though. The same old dreams would have replayed asleep in her room. But a volunteer in the Ground Observer Corp was trained to keep an eye on their town.

Umi must have been waiting for this chance to break from the park. She had to hurry to keep up with his rush down through the weeds and brush towards the water.

Crows bent the top of a leafless tree.

They crossed Holly in a run and Anita was glad the

trolley wasn't there.

A train whistled and anyone would have thought they were trying to catch it before it left the station. When they reached the pine stairway that led to the shore, she warned him, "Careful! The steps look slippery."

The damp air hummed and clanked with the presence of the nearby factory. Another loud hiss escaped it.

They followed the utility road along the harbor. Anita guessed they were headed for the fishing boats or the tall shape of a trawler.

As a truck passed them, Umi looked ready to dive into the blackberry that grew by the gravel. She put a hand on his arm and could feel how strong he was. The film cans must have been fifty pounds each. Even before the dust could settle, he carried them into the rumbling wake and Anita trotted to keep up with him.

The bay was blotted with patches of fog, thick in places as herds of sheep. She could only see the peak of Lemon Island. If his boat was out there, it was a ghost ship hidden in the mist. She imagined this mad retreat was to get him to an ancient fairytale galleon that had to bear him back to the seafloor. The handbook tucked in her bag didn't cover that.

She couldn't believe the dock he chose, they were nowhere near the tied fleet of fishing boats. The harbor still had relics from the last century, spindly narrow gangplanks that teetered out to where the sailing ships once moored. They were just wide enough for men carrying bales back and forth. By 1942 most of these makeshift piers had fallen apart, but many of the pilings remained, standing out from the waves in rotting rows. You could almost leapfrog your way to the sea.

A painted sign worried her: NO TRESPASSING but he bent around the gap of nailed scrap wood and was soon ten paces ahead of her.

Anita didn't see a ship waiting for him, unless there was a rowboat tied up out of sight at the drop-off end of the dock. The beach was fifteen feet below her, the tide crackling over barnacles and sharp rocks. She held the wet rail and called, "Are you sure this is safe?" Even if he stopped to hold up an index card, she wouldn't be able to read it.

Watching her shoes, she followed. He left his footprints on the dew. There was plenty of opportunity for her to fall through. The planks played out of tune like a broken piano keyboard. A few times she had to hop over jagged holes where the seawater hounded around the slanted pilings. "There ought to be a merit pin for this," she muttered. A little brass emblem she could wear next to her Aircraft Warning Service button.

Umi set the film cans on the last bit of dock and she saw him turn, climb down steps right onto the back of the fog. He was gone but there was no sound of a motor.

"Mr. Umi?" It took her some bravery to go all the way to the edge and peer over.

If a boat had been there, it was gone now. He stood just above the swell of green water, reading a ghostly paper scrap pinned to the ladder. When he tore it free she caught a glimpse of the writing. The creased top of his hat and his rumpled suit sleeves made her think of a man who lived in a shell, waiting for the tide to pull him back to the sea. Was it a note from a whale? Did it leave without him?

Anita took a step back from the drop. Her foot bumped the heavy film can and she read the tape on its side: Bob Hope.

CHAPTER FOUR

The Wind Creatures

His mother was the only one who called him Victory. They would talk at night when he stopped at The Leopold phone booth on the way to the wooden box he slept in. In the sixth grade he named himself Vatican Jones because he thought it made him sound like a movie detective. Now he went by VJ. Maybe next year he would change it to V. After that, he would fade from view.

The leaves above him chattered. He was on the path shouldering the creek. At first he supposed the wind was birds hopping around in the branches.

He remembered the story his mother loved to tell him, about the day she found the dead bird and met his father. It was real as a movie in his mind. He could see her in black and white film, in the 1942 world. She lit up when she talked about herself as a girl. Every early morning she walked across town to the chicken shack observation booth where she would watch the sky. Days of war and mystery. The radio had *The Shadow* and *Philo Vance*. Times were hard but people came together. She met Victory's father beside the bird's grave.

When VJ left the forest cover, back onto the sidewalk, he realized what made that sound on the leaves. He could feel it on his skin. It was rain.

He thought of his father, a sailor in the Imperial Navy invading a small town in Washington and stealing a Bob Hope movie for his submarine. He thought of the days and nights his father spent hidden in that chicken shack, using the radio to search the sea for another submarine from Japan.

The rain was gentle. It had just started to fall and wasn't sure if it would turn into more.

His mother volunteered in the Ground Observer Corp while willingly providing sanctuary to an enemy of the United States of America. It was hard to believe in 1992. She was in love with him. She held his hand when they went out in disguise to see movies at The Avalon. World War II was nearing its awful end and they were ghosts floating up Magnolia Street.

He heard the faint creak of snow geese somewhere overhead. They were headed for those big rain soaked fields south of town.

No wonder he was thinking of his parents, he wasn't far from the hill where they met. If only that broken clock tower of City Hall could talk. But what would it say that he didn't already know? She must have told him their story a thousand times. Hidden beneath the hillside under fifty years of weeds and wildflowers was the bird that brought them together. VJ wondered if he was that bird, reincarnated, and he laughed.

After three years his father disappeared like those geese. Did anything make any sense?

He wondered what his father would look like after all the years on the run. Would he ever come back here looking for his son?

The path followed the creek bank and rubbed along the concrete tanks of the salmon nursery. The water in the pools spotted with drops of falling rain excited the little fish below. They swam close to the surface and swarmed like silver. When the wind brushed across they shot below the water. He noticed the cycle start again as the rain peppered the smoothed water, attracting the curious fish until another gust of wind erased everything.

Down the path toward Holly Street, VJ heard someone laugh. Her laugh cut through the rattle and hiss of the trees bending in the breeze. It wasn't hard to tell who it was—she was one-in-a-million. 99 gathered a handful of leaves at her feet and tossed them in the air. Her laugh as they fell around her sounded like a rusty horn.

She was still picking them back up when VJ approached. He knew she wouldn't recognize him. They would go through the same vaudeville routine. His coat pockets were filling with the 99 Cent Store flyers. He stopped near her to get a few leaves she missed. When he offered them, she let him add to the pile in her arms.

"Do you know what I'm doing?" she said.

He was so surprised she had gone off script he could only shake his head in disbelief.

"Do you know about the wind creatures?"

"No," he croaked.

She said, "Look!" and shook the handful of leaves. "The creatures are invisible. But they travel in the wind when it's blowing. When I throw these leaves, you can see them. They're attracted to the falling leaves. Watch!" She bent her knees and tossed the leaves straight up in the air overhead.

They seemed to catch in the dusky sky, then as they fell he saw she was right.

Of course 99 would know about wind creatures. She spent every day on the sidewalk handing out paper, watching the way those flyers would fall when people tossed them. Sometimes a wind creature would carry a flyer half a block. And all those autumn leaves that would race along the concrete then skirl into little tornados. There was life in them.

It was a ballet. He could see the dancers only by the way the leaves moved with them.

99 laughed and took a step back to let them spin, close enough to her to be a dancing partner.

The leaves landed and were kicked around by the feet of those invisible creatures.

"Did you see them?" 99 asked. She was already gathering the leaves again.

So this is what she does, he thought. When she's not working, she has a whole other life.

He got a few leaves off the ground. They were still now, shed like feathers. "What are these creatures?"

She wore her pink hoody pulled around her face and she reminded him of one of those department store Easter rabbits. She had the same shambling gait as she bent to gather leaves off the path. "Creatures that live in the wind," she told him, "like birds or bats or dragonflies. Only bigger!" She laughed. "And they sure are playful!"

VJ agreed. When he offered her some leaves, she noticed the paper bag in his other hand. It made a clanking metallic sound.

She said, "Are you in the market for household items or hardware?" The change in 99 was that sudden.

"No. I had to go to Pacific Supply for some portholes."

"You don't want to pay top dollar for portholes. Have you been to the 99¢ Store?

"Yes, of course. Many times."

"Did you know nothing in the store is over 99 cents?"

"Yes."

"No games, no gimmicks."

He sighed, "Yes. I know."

"You'll find all your shopping needs under one roof."

Any second he expected her to hand him a leaf printed with advertising. It made sense. What better way to get the word out? Have every tree in town stamped in the fall and let the wind do its work scattering the leaves.

Finally 99 couldn't resist, telling him, "Let me give you a flyer," and she let go of all her leaves to search her handbag. If there were any invisible wind creatures around they were sitting still. They must have also known her routine by now. She was probably like one of the world's great clowns, appearing at dusk, under lamppost light at City Hall's park.

"Hey Vatican!"

He welcomed the distraction. He recognized his old friend on the sidewalk ahead. But before he could start that way, 99 fished out a green sheet of paper.

"We have lots of good deals today."

"Okay," he said, accepting it, "Thank you." Folded over, it went in his pocket with the others.

"No expiration date!"

"Thank you. I better get going now. Someone over there wants me." He took some steps towards Holly, then turned back. "Thanks for telling me about the wind creatures. I never knew about them before."

Of all the things to do, she saluted him. The leaves around her feet were scattered by a sudden breeze as the creatures carried them away across the grass. 99 was laughing again.

VJ's friend waited for him. The #3 bus went uphill in back of him, windows blazing like a steamship. "Well, well, well," the voice rolled from the street. "If it isn't Vatican Jones."

"If it isn't Socrates Nelson," he answered. He knew Socrates back when his name was Kevin. They both changes their names in the 6th grade. That was a busy day for City Hall.

"What brings you out in the wind and rain?" Socrates asked. "I saw you throwing leaves."

"Yes, just visiting with 99."

"99?"

"That's what I call her. She works for the 99¢ Store. She was telling me about the wind creatures. Do you know about them?"

Socrates shook his head. "I drove a city bus for forty years," he said. "I had all kinds of people tell me all kinds of things. In all that time nobody ever said anything about wind creatures."

"They're invisible."

"That figures," Socrates said, falling into step with him. "What way you going?"

"Back home. Somehow the day got away from me. I can't believe it's night already."

"Did you see the TV people today?"

"I don't have a television. There's no room in my boat for one."

"Oh brother," Socrates sighed. "They're filming a TV show over on Northwest Avenue."

"Really?"

"You know the show *Murder Conductor*?"

"I've heard of it."

Socrates explained, "Each week she goes to a different place and there's always a murder she has to solve."

A bright yellow square of light spread across the sidewalk like a carpet laid before them. They stopped on it and stared at the big display window. Sinbad's had filled the entire space of glass with a kind of aquarium wonder. A painted breadbox, a Yellow Bonnet coffee can, a clock with green jewels, a $29 Eastman camera, china serving bowls, ornaments and lights, a stack of LPs, porcelain bookends, a bucket of buttons, a photo cutout of Mae West draped with a feather boa, silver shoes, an Underwood typewriter, a secretary dresser for $80, a stuffed tiger, a globe on a stand, a red tricycle, a robot bank, a spoon on a thick diner plate. The wind made a move against them and Vatican let it lead him to the door.

"You going in there?" Socrates asked.

"I have to check something." The metal handle was cold.

"Yeah, well I've got a schedule to keep." Of course he did, he still held a bus wheel in front of him and rows of seats behind him with people waiting to get home. "I'll see you around."

"Okay. Bye for now." Seven steps ahead, the sound of the bell above the door wriggled like an eel in the air. Vatican reached over the plywood into the window display, past the lights and trinkets and he picked the dull looking spoon off the plate. It looked like it had shoveled coal on a Great Northern train.

Stamped along the handle, you couldn't miss the words: *Stolen from The Old Sea Gull.* He knew it was the same place his mother borrowed a spoon that fateful morning in 1942.

A white paper price tag rattled at the end of a thread. $5 seemed like a lot for an old spoon. Vatican smiled. Someone else must have known it was magic too.

The cashier was vacuuming. He imagined her constantly doing that. All that dust from ancient days was never ending. She stopped long enough to take his five dollars. The vacuum was going again by the time he reached the door.

No sign of Socrates.

Even without a bus Socrates still had a schedule to keep on Holly Street.

A gust of wind rattled the storefront window.

Somewhere along the way he became Vatican again without knowing exactly when. Having the name Vatican Jones again was a return to someone he knew in childhood, but also it was more. There was more to it than he could explain.

It was easy to picture the 12 year old Vatican Jones in the rain and wind of a sinister night. The streetlamp gave him a long shadow.

The spoon was a clue, but there wasn't much he could do about it at this hour. It was time to turn the corner and go home to Haiku. The wind ran beside him like a dog. It wanted to be the first in the door.

During the greater portion of a very busy life, I have been actively engaged in the profession of a Detective.

—from *The Expressman and the Detective*

Breakfast should be ready by now and he should be able to tell by the actions of other people whether they still saw and heard Martians.

—from *Martians Go Home*

CHAPTER FIVE

The Old Sea Gull

The rumbling passage of a freight train, the air horn screaming, wheels shrieking, felt like the planet was tearing apart but Vatican was used to it. The airplane scraps that made the walls of Haiku turned the box into a big teacup of noise.

Vatican's dream shook itself apart while he stirred. An eye opened and saw a sort of daylight. These cold winter mornings were slow to begin. Luckily, he slept with a spoon. That mystery would carry him out into the day.

The train rushed on along the bay but he could hear its fading whistle far ahead—two long, one short, one long—as it ripped across C Street, G Street and Bellwether Way.

An arm emerged slowly from the blanket and the rest of him followed. Standing up to get dressed, he could see over the hull of Haiku. The windows revealed an underwater murk. The dark shop was filled with the shadow stacks of airplane parts and sitting by the airframe in his overstuffed chair, Martin lifted an arm for a weary wave.

"That plane looks ready to fly," Vatican said.

"Yeah," Martin growled. "Once I put all the pieces together." He sat beside the quiet edge of airplane like an old frog and took a sip of coffee. "Once I finish it though," his breath made a cloud in the cold room, "I wonder what will be left for me to do."

"Then you go flying!" Vatican clapped his hands together.

"Where do you expect to go with Haiku?"

"Wherever it wants to take me."

Martin laughed. "Even if that crate does float, how's it going to move?"

"Oh…" Vatican paused. Somehow he pictured it just would. "Should I make a mast for a sail?"

"Why bother?" Martin said. "You should park it on the shore and put a roof with a chimney on it. A retirement home for old seagulls."

But Vatican was picturing Haiku sliding across the bay, the sounds of the creasing waves and the gulls crying around the big full sail. And then the louder noise of a 1917 seaplane flying overhead. Vatican waved from his wooden box at his imagination. "I can see it happening," he called over to Martin.

"Maybe," Martin said. The word made another cloud. "Maybe in the spring. Of course the weather never really gets good until mid-July."

Vatican buttoned his coat and reached for the ladder. His hands rested on it. "Did you just say old seagull?"

"What?"

"A minute ago. Have you heard of a coffee house called The Old Sea Gull?"

"Is it down by the dock where the tramp steamers tie up? Does the fog always blow around the door?"

Vatican climbed out of Haiku and took the spoon from his pocket. It had a pleasant weight, made of that prewar metal before everything was melted into weapons. "It was a café in the old Sunset Building on Holly Street."

"No. I never heard of it."

Vatican tapped the spoon on his hand.

"What is that you've got?" Martin asked. "A lollipop?"

Vatican crossed the shop, alongside the sparred wing. "This is a spoon from The Old Sea Gull. I think it might be a clue to my past."

"Really?"

"I'm going to do a little investigating."

"You're back to being a detective!" Martin held up his cup in salute. "The Return of Vatican Jones."

"That's right," he grinned, "I suppose it is." After so many years, he always felt the calling to be a detective again.

"Well, a lot's changed since elementary school."

"I know. This time it isn't about lost homework or secret Valentines. It's just one of those little ghosts of life."

"Oh, alright. Good luck then."

"Thanks."

Vatican was nearly to the door when Martin called, "I don't know if you're aware yet, but another detective just arrived in town.

Vatican turned.

"Shelby Wills."

"The TV detective?" Vatican asked.

"That's her. I hear she's pretty good."

Vatican laughed and put his hand on the cold door handle. "Don't worry, Martin. I don't think we'll be crossing paths. This isn't The Case of The Old Sea Gull Murder." Of course he was wrong about that.

Funny, he didn't even look at the clock, he just set out into the dark. It could have been the middle of the night. If he wasn't so intrigued by The Old Sea Gull spoon, he would have stayed curled up and covered in Haiku. That was the problem with imagination—it could get you into trouble.

Across the street and up the block, the lights of

The Old Crown shined on the corner. An old wind creature limped past him headed that way, scuffing a leaf off the curb. What sort of morning would begin without a cup or two of coffee?

Vatican followed the way the wind had gone. No cars were rushing down Holly but he wondered if those wind creatures could be run over. He had never bumped into a dead one, had he? What would you do if you did? Hang it on a clothesline and leave it to the breeze?

The dark shape of someone huddled on the bench in front of the café. Once the Lighthouse opened its door in the morning, they sent everyone out to roam. It was probably the same way with the wind creatures, Vatican thought. They slept on cots in some ragged looking cloud and were thrown down every dawn.

Nickels turned slowly at the sound of Vatican approaching. His guitar slanted next to him.

"Morning," Vatican greeted him. "Are you going inside?"

"I wanted to." A finger pointed accusingly from the sleeve of his army jacket. "Look who's in there instead of me."

Vatican observed the big yellow window and through the steamy glass he could see Pennies—heavy black overcoat, the big thick glasses of a blind man—holding his battered guitar and singing.

"My alarm clock didn't go off," Nickels groused. "I missed the bus. When I got here, I was too late."

"Do you want me to get you a coffee?"

"It's not about that! I came here to play Wobbly songs! Instead, I have to sit here and listen to him sing about it's only a paper moon!"

"Maybe tomorrow then," Vatican replied. It was

too cold—he had to visit The Old Sea Gull and he still wanted a cup of coffee for the road. He waved at Nickels who had become a slump on the bench again.

Pennies' voice carried through the opened door. He was down the ramp in the other dining room and it wasn't "Paper Moon." He was singing, "You are my sunshine, my only sunshine."

At this hour, Vatican had his choice of tables. He grabbed a copy of *The Wise Penny* and found a spot by the wall. Above him, a painting of a green hippo kept him company. He spread the paper flat and was turning the pages as a waitress appeared.

"Can I get you a coffee?"

"I would love that."

He went back to turning pages and was surprised—he made it all the way through the little newspaper without finding the crossword puzzle. Did they forget to print it? Did they run this half page ad for the Gary Justice used car lot instead? Vatican was searching the paper for a third time when the waitress arrived with coffee.

"Are you looking for a bargain?" she asked.

"I can't find the crossword. It used to be in the back. Look, they still have the horoscope, but no crossword."

"That's mysterious," she agreed. "Are the pages all there? Maybe that section fell out."

"Oh," he nodded. "That's possible." His coffee steamed beside his hand as he counted the page numbers. "No, they're all here."

She said, "Did you look in the Lost & Found section?"

Vatican could tell she was joking. You had to have a sense of humor. Where was the world without one? So what if *The Wise Penny* forgot to print the crossword, or worse yet decided nobody out there counted on solving that puzzle while they had their morning coffee. He folded the newspaper and was going to say something about taking out a Want Ad—"Wanted: The Missing Crossword"—but he realized she had already moved on to another table. She was refilling cups and laughing with them.

He took a sip of coffee.

It didn't taste the same. Yes…something was missing. It wasn't the same without the crossword.

He didn't even have his Issa book to read.

While he was watching the cook in the kitchen shaking a pan full of steam, the bells on the door rang as someone entered the café. Vatican also felt the cold of outside. He wondered if wind creatures ever came inside.

Nickels walked past the row of tables and when he stopped and glared at Pennies in the other room, Vatican expected an old Western shootout. For a moment the Mississippi John Hurt song froze in the air.

The waitress stepped in between them and addressed Nickels, "Good morning, neighbor. Can I get you started with a cup of coffee?"

Nickels sighed and turned his attention to her. "I'd like to order something different. Are you familiar with a half tea?"

She showed him to a table and said curiously, "A half tea?"

Nickels leaned his guitar against the chair next to him. "Yes. I don't want a full pot of tea at full price. I want half the tea leaves with all the hot water."

"So…you want a pot of weak tea?"

"Essentially, but it should be the equivalent in cost of a cup of tea."

"But it fills an entire pot."

Nickels nodded. "Right."

Vatican had to admit this was better entertainment than a crossword puzzle. The Old Crown was transfixed by Nickels' performance. Even Pennies had become just a song you would hear in the background on an elevator ride. Having delivered his show, by all rights Nickels should have earned himself a free breakfast.

The waitress must have thought so too. Or maybe she was just used to these early morning spectacles. "I'll see what I can do," she told Nickels.

"My eternal gratitude." Nickels removed his coat and sat with his back to Pennies. Even his guitar disregarded the music from the other room.

Vatican finished his coffee.

Nickels and his guitar had become statues. All that was missing was a pigeon and a tourist waiting for her picture to be taken.

Vatican wanted to leave a couple dollars on the table and be on his way. He was hoping to leave before Nickels asked him to pay for his half tea. Then he realized another predicament. He kept his money tucked between the last few pages of his library book. Without Issa, how was he going to pay for his coffee?

The waitress returned to his table with a Silex full of more coffee. "Refill?" she asked. She gave Vatican a look and rolled her eyes at Nickels and shook her head. "What a morning," she whispered.

"Ohhh," Vatican sighed. "You're not going to like this either. I don't know where my money went."

By this time, we have no doubt that the more inquisitive of our readers are beginning to be impatient to learn how we became acquainted with all these wonderful things.

—from *The Earth We Live On*

CHAPTER SIX

Coward's Corner

Even Nickels knew better than to end up in Coward's Corner. He might come in the door with only a dollar, but at least he had the sense to invent half tea. Not Vatican.

Vatican stood inside a painted border next to the garbage cans in the alley. This was a pretty good alley as far as alleys went—the cobblestones gave it a European look, shining clean from a night of rain—and he was sheltered from the wind. But it was maddening to know he was only four blocks away from where that Sunset Building once stood and The Old Sea Gull was waiting for him like a ghost. Still, he knew The Old Crown rules and the consequences if you disobeyed or broke them. Even the smallest thing like a cup of coffee could result in the punishment of Coward's Corner. Vatican couldn't leave until he served his time behind the yellow painted line.

Someone had chiseled marks on the brick wall behind him. Vatican didn't know if it represented minutes or hours. He had time to wonder.

A laugh from the other end of the alley surprised him. "What happened, Vatican?" Martin regarded him from the gray view of Champion Street. So close yet so far. "Doing time?"

"Did I leave my book back at the shop? On the edge of Haiku or somewhere?"

"What?"

"I keep my money in my library book and I forgot to bring it along with me."

Martin reached in his heavy winter coat and for a

moment Vatican thought he was going to reveal that paperback and his troubles would be over. Instead, Martin held an envelope. "Forgot to tell you...We got this from the library..." He also needed to find his glasses, tucked in his shirt pocket. After he settled them in front of his eyes, he read the letter aloud. "You have the following loan currently overdue. *The Year of My Life.* Fine 3 USD." Library books were free to borrow but God help you if you lost track of them. He shook his head. "You want me to fold this into a paper airplane and fly it to you?"

"No," Vatican sighed.

"You really got yourself into some trouble."

"I know, I know. I don't know where that book could be..." Vatican's morning began like Sam Spade with a spoon and a path to a place shrouded in intrigue and ended up prisoner in an alley. He never should have stopped for coffee. What kind of detective worries about an overdue fine? What kind of crime-stopping case was that? Vatican Jones and the Mystery of the Missing Library Book.

"You want me to bust you loose?" Martin asked.

"No...I better wait."

Martin held out his hand like a falconer. "Well, it's starting to rain."

"The rain will keep me company."

"Okay. I should get going."

Vatican waved from his painted line prison. "If you find that book, let me know. If not, I guess I'll have to follow yesterday's footprints."

Martin stuffed his hands into his coat pockets and nodded. A misty morning on the hills above town, the smell of the ocean, all it needed was a temple bell. "I'm off to see the TV show. Maybe the great Shelby

Wills can help you find that library book."

Vatican smiled. It was funny to think of her Sunday night show with millions of loyal viewers tuning into The Mystery of the Missing Library Book. "Anything's possible."

"I'll stop back here on the way home," Martin said. "If you're still here, I'll bring the cavalry."

Vatican saluted. He watched Martin drift out of the brick wall frame of the alley. The rain was coming down. It dripped along the telephone wires overhead. He pulled up the hood of his blue raincoat.

He could stay mostly out of the rain by leaning his back against the wall. A puddle was slowly filling, fed by the little streams running through the cobblestones.

How long was the sentence for an unpaid cup of coffee?

Where was that library book?

He wondered what Philip Marlowe would do… stuck behind a painted line in an alley full of rain…a lost book of Japanese poetry…and a fifty year old spoon in his coat pocket.

With a snap and squeak of hinges, a door opened on the other side of the alley. Vatican hadn't noticed it before. It looked like part of the wall. A black umbrella ducked through and when it tipped he saw a woman underneath. The umbrella and she looked like sisters—like they had played in the rain back when the Titanic sunk in the Atlantic.

Her shoes scuffed across. "My goodness," she said as she stopped next to him. The rain bounced off the umbrella's taut skin. "What on earth did you do?"

"I couldn't pay for my coffee."

"Here…" she said, passing him the umbrella, "Hold this for a moment, dear."

The big umbrella bristled inside with a network of tines but it felt light as a bird. It was easy to hold over both of them. The rain made a pleasant sound on it that reminded him of camping in a tent in the Cascades. With the memory of a mountain evening held overhead, Vatican watched her. She took a jam jar from a pocket in her overcoat, patted another place and found a paintbrush with a long wooden handle. In the next moment, she was unpainting the yellow line of Coward's Corner. Turpentine or magic elixir, whatever was in that jar made Vatican's prison wall disappear with every brushstroke.

"There!" she said and straightened back up. "Your troubles are over. You're free!"

He raised his arm to hold the umbrella higher until she put away her paints and could take the handle again. Passing it back, he told her, "I feel like I've just been saved by Wonder Woman."

She nodded. "Give me one good reason I shouldn't wear a cape." She laughed.

He couldn't think of a reason…He felt the rain again as she and her umbrella left…Anyone could wear a cape but not many did. She certainly deserved one. Bright red and blue and flowing behind her as she flew.

She crossed the wet cobblestones towards a rusty fire escape. Vatican was stunned. Where had that massive nautical-looking thing come from? Had a stage crew rolled it into the alley while she was painting?

Her umbrella pulled her to the stairway and she went up into the air like Mary Poppins. Each step rang like a dented bell until she stopped at the top where that same brick colored door had moved along the wall. She turned on the landing and looked at

Vatican. "I can make the rain stop too." She snapped her fingers and she was right. The air was squeezed dry.

Vatican took a couple steps away from the wall. Looking straight up at the sky, all he could see was a ghostly white. No rain. A seagull kited over the alley, looking down. Another train rumbled by the shore. Or was it the same one, running in and out of the ground on an endless loop?

He wasn't surprised to find she was already gone. That's what those heroic types always do. But he wished he could have said thank you.

With nothing to hold him in the alley, he let himself leave.

Out on Champion Street the cars were wet and the hill was slick as a river; all that remained of the rain. The City Hall weathervane pointed east, at the silvery disk of the winter sun. Every morning it climbed out of those dark forested hills, watched them all for a while as it rolled and took its time, dropping into the western seas.

Finally Vatican was on his way to The Old Sea Gull. Funny that so much adventure led up to that.

On the corner of Prospect, he waited for the traffic light to change. A crow was waiting too, watching from the top of the lamppost. When it blinked, the light turned green and Vatican discovered he had witnessed a secret. The crows were holding the circuits of the town, making everything come and go.

From the middle of the crosswalk, down the street to his left, he caught a glimpse of where the library would be. He patted his coat pockets as if that Issa book had magically returned. No such luck. There were only so many places it could be. It went with him to Pacific Supply, when he paid for portholes. Did it travel home after that? He remembered carrying the paper bag and meeting wind creatures in the park. It couldn't just disappear. It had to be somewhere along the path from yesterday.

He left Prospect behind, passed a window full of violins and a shoe repair shop. It wasn't much further to Railroad Avenue and up the hill to State Street. His mind time traveled back to 1942 and the blank winter sky was filled with the tall Sunset Building, rows of windows set in stone. On the ground floor, The Dream Theatre would be waking up in a while with a double feature. Above that were offices, small businesses and stairs to more. A dentist drill, typewriter, Tommy Dorsey. All that blinked out of sight as he stopped on the cobblestone alley next to the Columbia Bank.

A pair of shiny trolley rails remained. A big rhododendron loaded with buds ready to bloom. Fifty years ago his mother was here. Fifty years ago a three story building was here where the trolley ran, and she stopped at the door to borrow a spoon. Gone. A parking lot with Toyotas and Fords…A bank… Where was the air that had filled those floors? People breathed it in and breathed it out.

Vatican stepped over the curb onto the new coat of asphalt. He thought about going in to the bank and looking around but he had a pretty good idea what he'd find. A carpeted room, a counter, a guard giving him the eye, a row of tellers waiting for him to reach in his pocket…For what? He didn't have any money. All he had was a spoon that once belonged to the past. He considered the thought that maybe The Old Sea Gull still existed underneath, that maybe when they cleared away the Sunset, they settled the bank right on top of that café. The smell of pancakes still crept up through the ducts and the nickel jukebox sighed with Lester Young and Billie Holiday. There was no way to reach that coffee house anymore but you knew it was still there.

I am Deaf and I
made this bear
bookmark. Feel free
to buy this for any
price as you wish!

God bless you!
Thank you!

CHAPTER SEVEN

Poor & Unfortunate

Vatican followed the rails in the alley. They cut through puddles and pockets full of garbage carved into the cobblestones and patched concrete. After all these years he wondered how they stayed so shiny. Was there a ghost trolley? The rails stopped at the end of the alley where they ducked under the tar and cars. Magnolia Street. Funny to name a street Magnolia when all he could see was traffic and stores. Shouldn't it be a row of shimmering flowered leaves? Maybe that was how it used to look many moons ago. Or was it a vision of the future? When the world warmed, there would be a mile of magnolia trees and pools of warm clear water with manatees.

He waited for the light above the intersection to change. He missed his book. This was a good opportunity to read Issa. A few haiku to contemplate until he stepped carefully out into the road.

It felt like a dry riverbed. The cars and trucks were the current…sometimes a taxi…sometimes a bicycle, spinning like a leaf.

The rails reappeared in the alley on the other side, not as shiny, a little more ragged as if the trolley had gained rust crossing Magnolia.

Fifty years ago, his mother had gone the other way, towards the shore with her Japanese sailor. Vatican was leaving the memory. Another story lurked at the end of the alley. All he had to do was get there.

A crow flew from an open dumpster and startled him. Yes, these alleys had their own inhabitants, animals and people who passed through. Standing right on the worn-out tracks in front of Vatican, someone waited with a paper bag. His hand was tipped close to his ear, as if listening to the wind was all he could do. The ghost trolley would run him down if he didn't move.

With years of navigating alleys, Vatican knew the diplomacy. Like a captain in the Panama Canal, he raised his hand and gave a salute.

It sounded as if a parrot squawked in response. The man fumbled with his crackling bag and brought it to his mouth. He said something Vatican couldn't hear.

That same crow or one like it cawed from a crumpled gutter. It was watching them.

"Nice day," Vatican said.

The man spoke into his hand again. This time Vatican was close enough to hear, "Okay, I'll ask him." The thin sliver of a radio antenna extended from the paper bag.

Talking to a radio was nothing new. Vatican had seen his sort in alleys before. There used to be a guy with a teapot who would pour it for invisible friends. You had to play along until you got by.

"Hey mister…" said Radio Reality. "How would you like to be on TV?"

"TV?" Vatican humored him, "I thought we were on the radio."

"What? No—would—" He took a deep breath and tried again. Maybe casting for movie stars in an alley was a bad idea. "Listen, have you heard of *Murder Conductor*?"

Before Vatican could answer, the paper bag said, "Did you ask him? Over."

"I'm asking! I'm asking!" he told his walkie-talkie. The show always looked so peacefully done, with orchestra theme music that poured like treacle. Behind the scenes there was no end to the stress. "Look mister," he told Vatican, "we're filming a scene in this alley for the program. Do you want to be in it?"

Vatican shrugged. "It would seem that I already am."

"That's fine!"

Vatican watched him tell the radio, "The alley is secure. And I have a homeless person. Over." The bag crackled as he brought it closer to his ear.

"Okay," it replied. "We're on the way. Over and out."

"How about that?" he grinned at Vatican. "You ready to be on TV?" But he didn't wait for an answer—he was busy preparing for the crew.

Actually, Vatican Jones was no stranger to television. As a child he appeared with his Boy Scout troop on *The Count Misfit Show*. The studio was dressed as a gloomy castle. During the commercial Vatican watched the dry-ice fog cross the floor and then The Count invited them into the bright lights. He made a joke and fought with a bat that spun from the end of a fishing pole. Vatican got to wave at the big camera filming them and when the movie started again, The Count thanked them in an everyday voice. He gave them signed photos but who knows where time had taken them. Whenever Vatican went to Sinbad's, he would look for treasures that he lost.

"Okay, let's have you stand over here." With a last flourish, the man with the radio scratched a match and dropped it in an oil drum. Gray smoke crawled up out of it and brailed along the brick wall.

"What's that for?" Vatican asked.

"That's your fire." He scattered some tin cans and newspaper around it. "You're homeless. You live in an alley."

Vatican coughed.

"That's good! You can hold your hands over the heat." He said a word into his radio as he backed away. "I'm getting out of the scene now. Ms. Wills is on her way. You just stay there and act natural."

The smoke curled towards him and Vatican coughed again. What was burning in the oil can? Edgar Allan Poe's black cat? He didn't want to look. He held his hands out but they were cold now from being outside of his pockets.

Another train moaned down on the bay and he remembered *The Count Misfit Show*. He stayed awake til 11 that night, waiting for that haunted castle to appear. A Theremin ghosted like a train in the night, voodoo drums beat like boxcar wheels, as the buildup for the show began.

First, a bright white light stung the rippled alley stones and then the great TV detective Shelby Wills was there. She took her time as if all the world was scattered clues before her. It was funny though to see that trademark long purple coat, the crumpled hat on her head, exactly the way she lived on TV, only this was reality.

Vatican had to look away. He had to act natural. He didn't want to laugh.

Shelby Wills crept past with two cameras pacing her. The bright light swung with her when she took note of Vatican.

He held his breath. The cat had stopped burning. Cold poured from the can.

She paused next to him and said, "Here you are, my poor unfortunate friend." She dropped a coin onto his hand. With a cluck she left him, followed by her camera crew.

That was it.

Other people were talking, appearing around the corner in a caravan, carrying everything they needed to setup the next scene.

Vatican couldn't hold the coin any longer. He dropped it into his coat pocket. It left a round red circle on his palm like a burn.

"That was great!" The man with the walkie-talkie was back. "She even spoke to you! That wasn't on script." He put a twenty dollar bill on Vatican's branded hand. "Here's some spare change."

"Thank you." It still felt like there was a hot coal underneath that Andrew Jackson and the bill could burst into flame any second. Vatican stuffed the money in his shirt pocket. He needed to find a lump of ice to hold. He imagined ramming his hand into one of those hotel ice machines and the steam hissing up over his sleeve.

Once all the Hollywood people had gone, the only sound that remained was a birdish chirping. Vatican looked away from his hand and witnessed a small parade.

A girl pulled an old basset hound stuffed into a red wagon. The girl looked straight ahead towards the next street. The dog gave Vatican a baleful look. Its copper red rimmed eyes seemed to have seen it all. Anyone who watched Murder Conductor knew Shelby Wills' dog. It may have been slow as a bag of nails but there were episodes where that hound helped solve the crime. It didn't seem too interested in Vatican for now. That was liable to change. The chirping sound of the wagon wheels faded.

That was it.

Before Vatican left the alley he checked the oil drum prop to make sure the fire had gone out. That was the Boy Scout in him: "I promise to do my best, to do my duty to God and my country, to help other people and obey the law." He used to hold his hand up in a salute to recite that oath.

Down at the bottom of the drum was a half burnt stack of paper. If it had been anything else, Vatican would have let it be and be gone on his way.

He couldn't reach it without toppling in; he had to tip the metal barrel and claw for it. Too bad the camera had left, he thought, this would have been an award winning gritty shot. It was worth the trouble. When he crawled out, coughing and smudged, with another new burn on his hand, he held a copy of the script for this week's *Murder Conductor*.

As Vatican read the typeset, he could hear that gravelly voiced narrator's introduction: "America. A land connected by rails from coast to coast and everywhere in between run the trains. Past a farm, through a dark city, into woods and desert, they carry our dreams and they also carry the Murder Conductor."

"Excuse me. Is someone there?"

Vatican let go of the tipped oil drum and it gouged against the stones.

Another girl stood no more than ten feet from him. There was something other-worldly about her. It wasn't just her silent appearance, the vapory way she had come to the alley out of nowhere. She wore thick pastel winter clothes, a gray wool knit cap and large black glasses that made her face look like an ant.

Vatican glanced nervously behind himself and at the fire escape slung to the wall. Was she part of the show? Were the cameras still rolling?

She waited for him to do something. She held a thin slip of pink paper towards him. She knew he was there. "I am blind," she said, "and I made this bookmark. Feel free to buy this for any price as you wish."

"Oh," Vatican said. "Hello." He tucked the script under his arm and searched his shirt pocket. That was the only place he had any money, now that Issa was gone. "Here you are," he said, closing the distance between them.

Her somber face brightened with a smile. "God bless you! Thank you!" She didn't have any trouble taking the twenty dollars from his hand in trade for what she had.

Vatican slipped the bookmark into his empty shirt pocket. He didn't even have a book to put it in. He was poor and unfortunate, just like Shelby Wills had said.

That I am a singer of little songs,
proves that I have learned to read the world as a book.

—Milarepa

CHAPTER EIGHT

Dreaming of a Song

"Do you remember me? I was here yesterday."

"Of course!" The cashier smiled. "You were looking for portholes."

"That's right," Vatican grinned.

"Can I help you find something else?"

"Actually, yes. I was wondering if anyone turned in a book."

"A book?"

"A library book. I know I had it here yesterday. Now I can't find it."

She shook her head. The green parrot on her shoulder hunched and opened its beak as her gold earring swung near it.

"Do you mind if I look around?"

"Go ahead," she said and gasped. Her hands went up to pry the parrot from her earlobe. "Let go, Ignatius!" It clawed onto her hand, still gripping the earring.

"Okay. I'll retrace my path." Vatican backed from the register counter. He supposed pirates used to have her problem too.

Pacific Supply was in a hangar-sized building. A seagull could walk in and feel at home: anchors and fenders, winches, windlasses, buoys, outboard motors, life preservers and yellow vests. The speakers played the music of surf and terns. A fish tank full of salmon stared. Navy pea jackets, caps and lanterns. A big wooden steering wheel. Rain slickers, rubber boots and gloves, crab traps, rods, reels, a whole row of bait and lures, ladders, flags, hose clamps, bilge pumps, rigging and nylon cord. Canvas sail, paddles and gallon gas cans. A big spider web of seine netting hung from the ceiling. Vatican felt careful as a fly going around it. A bathysphere with a red SOLD tag tied to the hatch.

Vatican enjoyed the experience all over again. But there was no sign of the library book. He even peered in the narrow opened mouth of a giant clam. It only held the sound of the sea.

Finally, he had to assume Issa just wasn't here.

The book might have been picked up by a sailor bound for Japan, stuffed in a duffel bag halfway to Hawaii by now—there was no sign of it anymore.

Was Issa playing a trick on him? Did that old haiku poet want him to pace his little world back and forth and examine every detail the way Issa knew every bug and bending leaf of grass?

Vatican wanted to laugh and take it as a lesson, but every passing day that overdue library book was ticking like a taxi meter.

He supposed he must have brought it home and left it on the shelf in Haiku. Wouldn't that be a relief to see it again? And there was probably just enough money between the pages to pay for the fine.

When Vatican pushed on the door of Pacific Supply, he felt the cold winter air grab him like a polar bear and pull him outside. He stuffed his hands in his coat pockets and that coin Shelby Wills gave him brushed his knuckles. Once he was back home he would look at it with a magnifying glass. He was interested to know what kind of coin it was, what year and pictures and words were stamped into it. Maybe he would discover it wasn't a coin at all. Maybe that detective slipped him the washer from some haunted machine. It was interesting to think about as he crossed the parking lot for the sidewalk he knew by heart. Sometimes he wondered about those old Salish paths, if they had been turned into these sidewalks everyone used. Nobody seemed to remember. The city wanted you to think it had been here forever.

Vatican had a clear view of the bay. By Marine Drive a shiny train was left sitting like a toy. He supposed that was the one from the TV show. Didn't she have her own dining car? He imagined the cameras on her while the waiter served her hot soup in a bowl as white as the moon. She must have been examining the plot of some new murder.

Vatican thought about the soup. He hoped it was tomato. A thick buttered slice of sourdough bread was waiting to be dipped in. "My compliments to the chef," Vatican would say. The soup was so good he could feel it fill him with warmth. The holes in his clothes were steaming.

Shelby Wills pushed the entire roll of bread across to him. "Go ahead," she said, "help yourself to as much as you want."

Fresh hot bread, the kind you would smell when you passed the doorway of Avenue Bread. He held it in both hands and his fingers dug through the crust into the soft white. The waiter, or the butler, whoever he was in his tuxedo, set a cup of coffee next to that bread and Vatican was so deep in fantasy he almost walked right by Pennies.

"Hello?"

"Oh," Vatican said, back on a street corner. "Hello."

Pennies smiled. His eyes were those black glasses reflecting the world. The arms of his heavy wool coat wrapped around his guitar. He always seemed able to smile. It must have been those songs he played.

Vatican already knew there was no money in his pockets to give Pennies, but he went through the motions anyway. That's how he found Shelby Wills' coin again. Easy come, easy go. He tossed it in the cardboard shoebox. It made a loud plop like that frog in Basho's poem.

"Thank you. Anything you'd like to hear?"

Vatican thought for a moment. "How about Stardust?"

How many times could a jukebox play the same old song before the wax wore out? Pennies seemed to be getting there. His cold hands slipped on the strings and his voice cracked but the song was still strong enough to fly.

Vatican left that haunted melody to wobble around the lamppost on the corner until the guitar was done remembering. Halfway up the block, all Vatican could hear was the city sound, the cars, the chuff of the factory and another train on the way.

A strange time to go back to *The Count Misfit Show* but suddenly that memory returned. Their wooden TV was a direct line to the Count's castle. The Count had a flimsy projector, like the kind you could check out from the library. When it was ready, the reels would begin to spin and the square of light thrown on the stone wall would become a window into another world.

It was a town like Vatican's, a factory town beside the water. Boats went by, cars and trains. The tall smokestacks made dirty clouds that drifted in herds. Parents went to work, kids went to school. A boy woke up in the middle of the night and looked out his window. Across the steep slanted roofs, up and down and over the canyons in between, a strange loping creature moved. Its white fur glows with the moonlight. The title of the movie sprung so suddenly, young Vatican jumped. *Pongo By Night.* Only the boy in the film could see the white gorilla. It came to him with a warning message. Of course the ape couldn't speak, it had to show him. The boy put on his bathrobe and followed, raising the window, climbing on the mountaintops of houses, through the crowns of trees, over the flat tarred roof of the boy's school, all the way to the factory. The smoke blew through them. All you could hear was the rumbling breath of machinery. Pongo held the boy tightly at the top of a crane so he could observe what was happening. The hot ash that floated out of the chimneys, the sludge that poured from pipes, the sky that heaped in pyramids. It was worse than the Russians or the Martians, but nobody would listen to the boy—not his parents, his teachers, not the policeman he talked to. Vatican remembered the dreamy black and white way the TV seemed to float off the floor with the story of the boy and gorilla who climbed across all the rooftops to wake everyone and save the world.

Before he knew it, he was crossing Champion Street behind The Old Crown Café. Vatican didn't know what time it was, the sun was hidden behind dark cloudbanks and the clock on City Hall was always 7. If the café was still open, he would find out when he turned the triangle corner where Champion met Holly. He stopped there, shielded by *The Herald* vending machine. He didn't read the headlines. What did it matter what was happening in 1992? That was nothing compared to his escape from Coward's Corner. That could be a movie. He felt like one of those forgotten men on the run—leaving his crime behind for the nonstop jump on and off freight cars, the lonely time in hiding places covered by moonlight. Fortunately, when he glanced at the plate window, all he could see were the chairs up on tables. The only one left working was the dishwasher, mopping the floor. Some garage band cassette tape rattled the glass. Chain saw guitars and a thumping drum.

Vatican jaywalked when the road was clear. Down at the end of Holly, the Saint Paul's church wore a pointed winter steeple. A pigeon took off from the sidewalk in front of him and headed that way.

Vatican decided it was best not to look in Sinbad's window. He still had that spoon in his pocket. What was he supposed to do with that? The Old Sea Gull was long gone. Maybe he could bury the spoon in the ground like his mother's 1942 bird. What would she tell him to do with it? He guessed it was time to call her again and find out.

Not yet though.

First, some tomato soup from a tin. Vatican was a fantasy away from Shelby Wills' dining car. He didn't have a butler to turn the can opener, or stir the pan on the hotplate, or serve it with a folded linen napkin. He did have her script though. And he would soon know more about the story than he knew before.

CHAPTER NINE

Goodnight Haiku

"Where's Haiku?"

"What?"

"Where's my boat?" Vatican asked.

Martin stood up to get a better look. He watched Vatican run to the empty space by the wall. Had someone stolen it right from under his nose?

"It's gone!"

"How? All I did was take Gertrude for a walk to the park. We were only gone for a while."

"I don't know…" Vatican's detective eyes searched the floor, but he didn't see any clues…no footprints, or scratch marks, or tracks left by wheels. Nobody dropped a matchbook printed with the name of a saloon.

Martin was baffled. "How did they get it out of here? The door is too small and I keep the sliding one padlocked."

Vatican took a deep breath and sighed.

Martin said, "What if they took it apart? They could carry it out in sections."

Vatican turned the handle on the wall and opened the door. He hoped he would see Haiku sitting outside on the gravel, set near an ice cold puddle. There was nothing out of the ordinary. It was calm as the photo of the sky where a cloud had come and gone.

He stood there for a minute just trying to fathom what had happened. The shadow of some giant bird swooped through and carried Haiku away.

"I don't see anything else missing…" Martin said behind him. "The plane is here, the tools, my favorite chair…"

"Did they leave the hotplate?"

Martin looked back along the wall and saw it sitting there like a turtle. "Still there."

Vatican couldn't take his eyes from the gravel. He seemed to be listening to that crowd of stones. Was there one little pebble that would tell him what it saw? "Is there still a can of soup next to it?"

Martin looked again and confirmed there was.

From the north side of the bay a train was making its way closer. It felt like it was bringing a hundred cold cars full of snow. Someone somewhere today said something about a cold front coming from Canada. Vatican didn't want to be standing there so close to the tracks when it crashed into town. He shut the door behind himself and turned the lock.

He stared at something that wasn't there.

Over and over it seemed he was taught that lesson. There was nothing to hold onto when you are living in a dream. He started towards where he could still imagine Haiku. He thought about Ryokan who would have turned this into a poem: when a thief stole from him, there was still the moon left in the window. At least Vatican had his hotplate and soup. That was some small comfort.

While Vatican was stirring the pan, Martin returned. He was carrying a heavy folded cot. It looked like it had served on the frontline in the Civil War. It received an honorable discharge in 1863 after the Gettysburg Address. Martin set it by the wall where Haiku had been. "You can use this if you want."

Vatican nodded. "Thank you, I will." But he knew he was in for some strange dreams sleeping on that contraption. "You want some soup?"

Martin shook his head no and said, "I can't get over it. Nothing else is gone. Someone just wanted your boat. Should we tell the police?"

"No," Vatican replied. He held the pan by the long silver handle. The soup was red as flannel. "I'm a detective, remember. I'll find it."

"It sure is a mystery."

"I know."

"I don't even know where you would begin."

"With soup," Vatican said and he dipped a spoon in.

Martin's response was lost in the roar and scream of the southbound train. When they went by this close, any conversation would have to stop. Whatever words you were stringing along would have to wait like the traffic stuck at the crossing, watching the storm of it pass in the windshield.

That train gave Vatican time to eat his soup. It could have come with instructions on the can: *this soup will last one train long.* All that time he kept thinking of Shelby Wills and her calling him poor and unfortunate and he wasn't. She was wrong. He still had hot tomato soup. He had a cot and this big safe roof to sleep under. If it snowed tonight he wouldn't have to worry. There was nothing left in his pan but some red and the train was gone.

Sometimes when it was quiet he realized he was just waiting for the next train.

Vatican brought the pan to the sink and filled it with water to soak. He was too tired to wash it. That cot was calling him. He wasn't going back out into a night about to snow, to use the phone booth in the basement of The Leopold. He could ask his mother about the spoon another time. That could wait.

When he sat on the cot, it felt like the cloth wing of Martin's airplane. The pine slats creaked. He would be a 1917 pilot all night long, trying to keep himself in the air. The motion of sliding out of his coat caused a chain reaction of more snaps and creaks. He missed his bed in Haiku. This would be like sleeping in the branches of a bare winter tree.

The rolled up script fell out onto the green canvas like a newspaper thrown on a lawn. *Murder Conductor*, Season 5, Episode 2, "Island Air." Some of the pages had been torn out. He guessed those scenes had already been filmed. The story was in progress, the scene was familiar, an alley where detective Shelby Wills was searching for someone.

"Is she looking for me?" Vatican wondered and turned the page to find out.

The alley led her to a café. Anyone who watched the show knew she had a fondness for pastries. It would be impossible for her to walk past. If she had to plant a clue in there just to get her in the door, she would. And sure enough, while she was savoring a plate of rhubarb pie, someone burst on the scene to announce there was a dead man in the alley. Fortunately Shelby Wills was on her last bite. It was written in the script that way.

She set her spoon down and led the way outside. It was snowing. A crowd gathered around her as she kneeled beside a dead homeless man. On his open hand rested a black coin.

The rest of the script was burned away.

Vatican supposed that's where the show would have gone to a commercial anyway. He set the script on the floor beside his cot. He was so tired. That warm tomato soup had done a number on him. He yawned.

All he wanted to do was sleep and forget the whole day. Tomorrow was a new one. He hoped it would be better. The cot complained as he lay down. He closed his eyes and sleep didn't take long.

The custodians in his dream were just finishing up mopping the edge of a pond. They had to get the cattails to look just so. With barely a hum, a fog machine covered the ground with a low misty cloud. The sound of a battle clashed in the distance. Vatican heard horses and cannons and gunshots snapping, a dull surf-like roll of the armies and screams here and there. Vatican knew the man in front of him who stood with his back to the battlefield. The leaves made a curtain behind him. He sipped from a tin cup. He wore the familiar black suit and a stovepipe hat. A 3rd grader would recognize him. Why was Vatican visiting Abe Lincoln? 1992 was a century away. Then Vatican remembered the cot. It was happening just the way he thought. That ancient bed was telling him its story. Its voice rattled on like a wooden telephone. Everything it said, Vatican could see. Restlessly, he turned from the Civil War and as he did, he knew he was back on that cot. It wasn't like sleeping inside the walls of Haiku.

He could see the gloomy shapes of the airplane across from him. The wings were stacked like movie screens. A car on Holly Street lit the ceiling as its headlights raked along the rafters. It never got very dark in this big room at night but Haiku used to keep him sheltered from sight.

He didn't know what time it was. Haiku had a nice clock with a round green glowing face. It was comforting if he happened to wake in the middle of the night. 2:27, it would say, calm as the moss on a river stone.

He moved a little and the cot argued. He couldn't tell if his right arm was still asleep or if he took a bullet in that dream.

After all the time he spent building Haiku, Vatican was hollowed out. Despite the protests of the cot, he rolled onto his back and stared at the ceiling. He had such plans…he wanted to bring Haiku to the harbor with the help of a few people to carry it and set it in the seawater. Maybe Pennies could be persuaded to play a song. Once Vatican got in, he would wave over the edge and if nobody minded he could recite a poem. How would he leave the shore? Would he have oars or motor, or would it be a sail? A sail would be best. It would be a sunny warm day with just enough breeze to fill the bright orange cloth. Then he would slowly drift from the shallows. The factory noise would fade until water and wind were the only sounds. He might lie down for a while and be mesmerized by the framed blue sky. 5 x 7 feet wide. That had always been his dream. It didn't matter where Haiku would take him.

The headlight glow of another passing car flew across the room like a white owl.

Vatican sat up and set his feet on the floor. The cot threatened to wake the dead until he stood and let it be, like a mousetrap left armed to snap.

The Sea of Tranquility was quiet. Martin was asleep in his room in the corner. Spade & Archer was painted on the pebbled glass, just like in *The Maltese Falcon*. That was Martin: he clung to those old things America rolled over.

The Curtis Seagull was another of them, an ancient airplane stuck in a pool of shadows.

Vatican walked over to the window. Holly Street

wasn't much to look at. Or maybe it was. It depended on how you looked at it.

It looked like a dark sea had washed over Maritime Drive, filled the train yards and tracks, gone right up the sides of warehouses and parked cars and climbed the slant of Holly. Were the windows of The Sea of Tranquility underwater too? The streetlamps hazed pearly greenish light. The parking lot off Champion shined with orange anemone. Kelp strung the telephone poles. A pilot whale the size of a Chevrolet slept at the curb.

Vatican was enjoying the sight, like someone staring from a submarine, when he saw two people cross the street. The one on the left was big as a gorilla. He looked like he could have picked up the cement corner of the street to let all the water out. The one on the right was another story. Vatican recognized her. Anyone who watched TV in America would know her. She could have walked right out of her show, the latest episode "Island Air." But why was Shelby Wills strolling about at night with a circus giant?

CHAPTER TEN

Another Mystery

Vatican woke up to Chinese mountains. Steep green mountains heaved up like soft blanket folds, trees placed here and there, alone or in crowds, little temples, paths with wandering monks, hillsides tilled by farmers, rivers and creeks that spilled waterfalls into valleys below, children chasing a cow, mysterious white clouds that made land vanish, a lonely pine that tilted over the cliff like someone ready to fall or about to fly. Everything that was going on was frozen for a moment, waiting to start again. The wheels of the oxcart wanted to turn. Daylight glowed across the scene like a movie screen. It wasn't a dream though, or some strange cartoon. It was painted on four folded panels. Nothing was actually moving in it. The world held its breath. His eyes lingered on the black bird on a tree branch. Its song was stuck in the air.

Vatican's nose was cold. The room was cold. The cot cursed and wobbled as he moved beneath the heavy blanket. He heard the 20th Century outside on the street: a bus and cars, an airplane, a train, a crow cawing like a saw and he could see his breath leave him like a cloud. There was no more point in trying to sleep. He yawned and rode an avalanche out of bed.

How cold was The Sea of Tranquility? He could hear the heaters were turned on, but there didn't seem to be much difference between here and outside. He quickly slipped into his jacket and pushed his feet in his shoes. He was hobbling around with that when the door to the street cracked open.

"Ahah!" Martin boomed. "The sleeper is awake!

How did you fare on that cot?"

Vatican rubbed his sleeves and said, "It's so cold."

"Well, I've brought something to make you warm." He held a cup of coffee in each hand. Gertrude shambled around him and shook.

"Is it snowing?"

Martin pointed at the window, "See for yourself."

Vatican stepped around China and saw Holly Street. Like the white clouds on the painted screen, anything touched by snow was vanishing: roofs and rough edges, parked cars, ledges. Snowflakes no bigger than dimes were falling. "I had a dream it was snowing," Vatican remembered.

"That dream was real." Martin and his boxy dog headed for the rocking chair planted beside an orange space heater. Another chair was set there too. "I put that privacy screen up while you were sleeping. Beats sleeping out in the open."

"Yes, thanks. When I woke up, I thought I was in a different world."

Martin laughed and said, "Come have some coffee. You'll never guess what happened at The Old Crown."

"Did they find my book?"

"What?"

"My library book. I spent all yesterday looking for it."

"Oh…no. I don't know. I didn't ask about that. Here—" he passed Vatican a paper cup. "Have a seat."

Gertrude was flopped before the floor heater with her eyes closed. Going to the café and back was a day's work.

"All those TV people were having breakfast over there."

Vatican remembered seeing Shelby Wills and

her pet gorilla during the night. His hands wrapped around the hot cup.

"Someone asked me about Gertie and then about me and before you know it, I told them about our place which it turns out they already noticed. They were curious about the seaplane. They liked that story a lot and all of a sudden, Shelby Wills herself tells me they'd like to film it for the show. *And...*" he took a sip of coffee, nodded and continued, "They're going to help get the plane flying! That will be the ending for the show!"

"But you can do that. You don't need them."

"No," Martin shook his head, "I tried. I tried. Can you imagine a whole TV crew in here? With that kind of help we can put the plane together in no time."

Vatican took a drink and looked at the cracked crown stamped on the paper cup.

"Shelby Wills mixed me right into the plot while I was standing there!" He raised his cup, "And they're going to pay me too."

"Oh boy..."

"Hey! I can pay off your tab at The Old Crown!"

Vatican couldn't help laughing.

Gertrude thumped her tail.

"To be honest," Vatican told him, "I've already appeared in their episode. They caught up with me when I was cutting through an alley yesterday."

"Really? How did that go?"

Vatican shrugged, "Strange." He remembered the coin Shelby Wills dropped on his hand. Now he wished he didn't give that to Pennies. There was something wrong with it.

"Wow!" Martin marveled, "This whole town is getting in on it." He had some more coffee and said,

"Did they pay you?"

"Twenty dollars."

"Twenty bucks!" Martin was flabbergasted. "You can live like a king for a day!"

Vatican shook his head. "I gave it away to a blind girl." He patted his coat pocket. "She gave me a bookmark."

"Twenty bucks for a bookmark?"

"Yes."

"Well, I hope that comes in handy for you. I hope it can turn into a life raft if you fall off a boat."

Vatican laughed and old Gertrude's tail wagged again. He reached over and gave her a scratch. As usual she was blocking the heater and her fur was like hot straw. That was how she spent these cold months. She closed her eyes and went back to a dream. "Good dog," Vatican said.

"What do you suppose she's dreaming about?" said Martin.

They looked at her paws flicking the air. Vatican said, "She's running after something."

"Probably a rabbit." Martin finished off his coffee. "She used to love that."

There were rabbits in the neighborhoods across the street, on the way to the park. After all these years, Gertrude would still be on the lookout for them. Vatican wondered if they were easier to catch in dreams. Probably the same…And that reminded him of his own predicament: running around with a 1942 spoon, searching for an overdue library book and his stolen Haiku. "I should get going too, before I start looking for something else that can't be found." He stood up from the chair. "Thanks for the coffee though." He still had half a cup.

It wasn't easy to leave the heater and the sleeping dog; it would have been nice to sit there and watch the window falling snow. But he had things to do.

Outside, the parking lot was a thin white sheet of paper. Some bird tracks were typed onto it.

Vatican liked the sound his shoes made on the snow. Other footprints like his had come and gone on the sidewalk. He glanced at the café across the street and wondered if all those TV people were still in there, plotting out the day's script. He hoped he wasn't a part of it. It might be interesting to listen in, but Vatican knew he couldn't set foot in The Old Crown without money. And all his money was in a missing library book that was probably lost in a missing boat. What a chain of events…As he walked he let himself wonder if they were connected somehow.

He turned left on Holly Street and added fresh prints to the morning path. The town seemed quieter than usual, muffled by the snow. The factory steamed. He walked downhill in the wake of the café breakfast smell. His stomach gave him a push but he wasn't going back. How could he eat? He didn't have a penny and Coward's Corner in the snow wasn't where he wanted to be.

Besides, he already had somewhere to go. Back in the shadows last night, Shelby Wills and her backup were leaving along Central Ave. They were coming from the waterfront. If that wasn't suspicious, he didn't know what was.

The snow covered their trail but he had seen them. It wasn't a dream. He slipped a little on the corner as he bumped into a cold breeze. It whirled and guarded its spot. He supposed there were different species of wind creatures. This one preferred the bitter cold.

He would love to ask 99 if that was true. He smiled thinking of her reaction to his questions. Were there other wind creatures that lived in hot climates and rode in those funnel dust devils? And what about Dorothy in Kansas? Wasn't her house carried by wind creatures to Oz? Was it possible to travel with them in the wind? 99 would stare and stare at him…Then she would hand him all her flyers and give him her job. You don't have to be crazy to work here, but it helps!

Central Avenue dead-ended at the railroad tracks and Vatican crossed them carefully. The rails gleamed sharp as knives. A seagull ran away from him. He followed the narrow path overlooking the water. There were more footprints. Other people and a dog had been this way today.

He had to walk over the train bridge and he had a good view of the estuary below. The creek emptied mountain water into the bay. The land crumbled over the grassy edge. Litter lay half buried or rusting. Someone slept under the bridge, just above the high water mark. It couldn't have been an easy place to rest, especially with the trains going overhead every half hour or so. But it was calm right now. Low tide. Gray pools were left like scraps of winter sky. A blue heron picked its way slowly over the mud.

Vatican didn't want to be on the bridge if a train was coming; there was no way of knowing until you heard its horn. He hurried along.

The loud outboard of a little crabbing boat bounced toward Lemon Island. The Salish Sea stretched all the way south, past Seattle. It was filled with green islands, salmon and whales. He heard it compared to the Inland Sea of Japan. Vatican had never been there but when he was inclined to think of his father, he thought he might have come from there. Would he have found it similar? The same sort of trees and clouds and water.

In the old days there were a lot more docks and jetties but in 1992 they were almost all gone. They left piling reminders out from the land where the canneries once stood. Offshore was like a graveyard with tombstones leaning out of the waves. Some poked from the water just enough like a seal taking a breath.

He was glad to make it back to land, to where the path picked up again and took him away from the tracks. Between bare blackberry vines and a chain-link fence the path was like white sand. Nobody had been through here this morning. That didn't mean Shelby Wills wasn't here before it snowed. She would have walked by this same factory yard where they kept rusted spare parts, some choice bones that rose from the ground like a mastodon kill. He didn't see Haiku in that zoo.

It had stopped snowing, those snowflake dimes were done falling through a jukebox of air to make the song of a cold factory and three seagulls crying above. The birds were circling like a big record playing. They made such a racket Vatican turned his attention their way. They spun over the end of a rickety pier. It looked like it had been penciled from land.

Vatican felt he was looking at that same pier his mother visited in 1942, as if it had been drawn there from another time. Something else he saw made him hurry. He slipped when he began to run towards shore. He didn't have the best shoes for the weather.

The pier was gated and a red and white sign warned: CONDEMNED. That didn't matter. Vatican crawled over the wooden slats and dropped onto the fresh snow. No other footprints, just some holes where the boards were broken through. He kept his hand near the railing. The pier tipped like a wooden rollercoaster track. One slip and he was underwater with the ghost of his father's submarine. A more careful person would have taken their time on the pier, or wouldn't have walked onto it at all.

Vatican's eyes were fixed on something at the very end. One mystery was solved: Haiku was roped to the last dock piling. She listed badly and she had taken on water, but there she was. Just like in his dream only she had sailed without him. He didn't know how, but that didn't matter. Another surprise and another mystery waited for Vatican. As soon as he got a little closer he would see.

CHAPTER ELEVEN

The Old Pond

Pennies floated face down in a foot of seawater. Vatican recognized the clothes and the guitar that lay half drowned beside him. There was snow on his back.

The tide must have left without him or maybe it was returning him to land.

Vatican put a hand on the ladder. It wobbled. The nails holding it to the barnacle covered pier were soft. They would snap, wouldn't they, if he tried to descend? Then he would fall into the same wooden box as the dead street singer. Is that what happened to Pennies? Last night, did he see Haiku and try to climb the ladder down into its bed? Vatican didn't think so. Pennies was no fool...He knew how to survive...Or at least he used to.

Vatican wished it was the scene from a bad dream but it wasn't. Nothing changed when he shut his eyes and opened them again. Why did Haiku have to be part of something so awful? He retraced his footprints down the pier to the safety of the shore. He looked back once before he set off towards the marina.

With a whoosh, all of a sudden it seemed that sound returned. The factory let out a shrill sigh. A crow cawed. Another train was on the way.

Pennies should have been at The Old Crown right now playing "Avalon." What had gone wrong?

A real detective would have been looking for clues. A real detective would have hauled Haiku to shore and gone over every inch of it. Vatican supposed he needed to get a real one. The marina had a telephone.

Walking fast, watching his feet, he stepped over a

row of deer tracks.

The snow made it seem like an empty world.

The train was coming. The dull heavy thump of the rails and metal squeal.

He hoped the deer was far away by now.

Along the edge of the water, beside a ten foot willow tree in a pot, was another place he could stop. It was better than walking all the way to the marina to find a payphone.

A drift of smoke left the chimney on top of a houseboat shack. A black wire strung down to it from the air. That meant they had a telephone.

The train was getting louder. He was used to the sound. It meant almost nothing to him.

Rhododendron leaves. A sign posted next to them read: THE OLD POND.

Vatican didn't know if it meant what he thought: Basho.

Another wooden sign just before the ramp leading on deck told him more: Tea House. He never saw this place before, but new things were going up all the time. Vatican's breath stuck to the air like wool. Behind him, the train roared.

If any frogs were jumping in ponds, you couldn't hear them.

Vatican crossed the shallow water on planks. His reflection wore a starfish and a seaweed coat. Minnows darted out of his way. What did they know? Enough to stay alive.

All he was thinking about was the telephone, the call he would have to make. Pennies was dead.

The wet and frozen deck of The Old Pond crackled underfoot. A cedar tree grew in a bucket beside the door. Vatican knocked. It didn't seem quite real, as if he was waiting for some fairytale animal to appear. He turned the handle and opened the door. If it was a dream, he stepped right into it.

Vatican let white winter light fall in a candlelit room. He knew he was disturbing a quiet place, but he had to report a murder. Was it a murder? It felt that way. "Can I use your phone? I have to call the police. There has been a death."

A dark haired woman sitting at a table pointed at the wall. There were only three tables in the room, two round windows, a wood stove with a pan of steaming water. A black telephone clung like a bat to the shiplap.

While he hurried to it, she stood and went to the stove. Customers were rare. Sometimes it seemed they didn't even know they were here. And so, while he dialed and told his story to the police, she went about her work. She made him a cup of tea.

First she opened a ceramic jar and scooped out a portion of bright green tea powder. She measured that into a smooth bowl-like cup, adding a splash of hot water, whisking and pouring in more water until it foamed like a tidal pool. By the time Vatican was done with the phone, she had the cup of tea waiting for him at the table.

He sat down across from her. "I'm sorry for that. I feel I fell in your door. Like a derailed train."

She said, "I made you some tea. This will make you feel better. It's peaceful in here."

"Thank you very much." He wrapped his hands around the cup. "I don't know how it happened. Someone I know died." He held the cup and looked at the bubbles. "It's a dew drop world," he sighed. "You remember that haiku? Issa says it all."

The taste of green tea and the rhythm of The Old Pond calmed him. They didn't need to say anything and he was glad for that. They listened to the water bubble on the stove. In a while she got up and carried his empty teacup to the sink.

For another minute or so, the room stayed calm.

Then the door swung open. A flash of white and cold air. Vatican shielded his eyes and blinked.

The silhouette framed in the doorway was Shelby Wills. This was exactly the sort of arrival you would see on TV. She entered the room followed by two policemen.

"Hm," she huffed, inspecting the room with a glance. For a second her eyes stopped on the woman and she said, "I'll have a coffee, dear, when you get a chance."

Vatican watched her near and he felt guilty as one of the villains on her show.

She slid out the chair opposite him and sat down.

"Did you make the phone call to the station?" she asked.

"Yes."

"And it was you who found the victim in that crate?"

"It isn't a crate," Vatican said. "That was my home."

Shelby Wills nodded with a terse smile. "Yes, I suppose that's better than a cardboard box."

"Someone stole it from me yesterday."

"Is that so?"

"And I bet the person who stole it is the one who killed Pennies."

Shelby Wills turned slightly in her chair to accept the saucer and coffee cup. "Thank you, dear."

"I went looking for my boat first thing this

morning," Vatican continued. "I called the police as soon as I could."

"Sounds like you know the victim, hm? You said his name is Pennies?" She paused long enough for a sip. "And why do you call it a boat now? I thought you said it was your home?"

"It's both. I was living in it on land until it was ready to become a boat. That's been my dream all along."

"And did poor Pennies know about your dream?"

"No. I barely knew him really. We would meet on the street. He played guitar and sang. That's how he made his living."

Shelby Wills took a long slow drink of coffee and set the empty cup on the saucer. She stood and leaned across the table and spoke in a sandpaper whisper only Vatican could hear, "I remember you. I gave you a coin yesterday. A black coin. A marker. That was meant for you, but you passed it on to another man—one who died—who died for you." She rapped the tabletop twice and added sternly, "You won't get away."

As Vatican sat there stunned, she straightened and called to the two officers next to the door. "Okay Captain, I think we're ready to go. But we'll stay in touch with Mr. Jones here." She shot him a look. "We wouldn't want you floating off."

"How did you know my name?"

"Oh! Didn't I tell you? We found something of yours at the murder site." She dug a book out of her shoulder bag and dropped it on the table next to him.

Of course he recognized it: *The Year of My Life*.

"Your name is on the checkout receipt." She started to leave then she stopped. "You know being a member of society does come with certain responsibilities, Mr.

Jones. Fortunately there's enough money stuffed in the pages to pay for your overdue fine." She served him a pressured smile, one of those cold handshakes she would deliver every show to the criminal who thought they were getting away with something. With that, she left. White watery light splashed across the tabletop.

Vatican felt the cold before the door snapped shut again. He stared at the library book. If only it had been a camera instead, recording this last day of his life. It would have been able to show him pictures of everything that happened.

He wasn't given much time to think about it. The calm of the room began to disassemble. Two long rows of white light fell across the table from the ceiling. Then, with a wrenching cry the entire wall facing the sea collapsed. The other three walls swayed and waved like sheets on a wash line. He saw a crane in the open sky lifting off the roof like a lid. The outside world was returning.

In another moment, the tables were gone and he sat in a chair at the edge of the shore. Pretty soon that vanished too and he was sitting on a seaweed covered rock. The Old Pond was a memory.

"I thought I detected a funny kind of resemblance to somebody I used to know."

—Clark Gable in *Idiot's Delight*

"Why did you let me go? Why did we have to go through all this nonsense?"

—Barbara Stanwyck in *The Lady Eve*

CHAPTER TWELVE

The Shirelles

Vatican still held the library book. That was the only prop left from the set of The Old Pond. The film crew carried everything else out to waiting trucks on the other side of the tracks. Was he just plunged into their TV episode, or did Shelby Wills really mean what she whispered in his ear? Pennies was dead, wasn't he? Was she trying to pin the murder on him? Had she threatened him with death too? Vatican didn't know anything except that it was freezing sitting on a barnacled rock. He heard a train coming or going. The TV crew had left him with that sound.

He stood up and made sure his footing was good. The beach was covered with stones of all sizes. All he had to do was knock one aside and the little crabs would scatter. They were waiting out this dream for the tide to return and cover everything in water.

Across the bay, the island trees wore snow. It was cold here too. He slipped Issa into his jacket and rubbed his hands together. To his left, with the factory in the background, that spindly dock leaned in the gray. He didn't see Haiku. The police must have pulled it ashore and taken it away. Pennies was probably laid out on a stretcher. There would be a couple sentences about him in *The Herald* tomorrow: "…a guitarist who made our streets his home since the 1980s died yesterday. A memorial service is being scheduled." And what about Haiku? Could Vatican really get back inside and make that his home after what happened? The sea hissed on the shore, a little closer with each breath.

Vatican turned from the shore and headed up the slick hill back to the path he arrived on. It was slushy and slippery now after the TV crew took The Old Pond away. Their tracks trampled around the blackberry towards the parking lot on West Myrtle. Vatican chose a different path.

Was this really what he wanted when he began his detective career in 6th grade as Vatican Jones? A jumbled mystery of clues and crimes and on top of it all, he was suspected of murder. Or was he in line to be murdered?

A single snowflake landed on his face. That must have been the loneliest snowflake ever. It woke up late, missed the blizzard crowd, but threw itself off the cloud anyway, tumbled head over heels down, down, down only to crash against Vatican.

He retraced his footprints on the snowy path. The chickadees bounced around in the brush. At the factory yard, he veered off along the Cyclone fence and made his own trail. A junco took off in front of him.

Vatican tried to make sense of what happened.

It wasn't all bad.

First of all, he found Haiku.

Second, his library book was back.

He even had money to pay the fine.

He ought to feel good about that.

More deer tracks passed ahead of him. They were probably from the same deer he saw before. After it visited the shore, it crept towards the woods for the day.

Then he remembered the way things went wrong. An unexplained death and a death threat. Worse yet, the more he thought about it, was any of this even real?

Was it all just the plot of a TV detective show? Let's face it, he told himself, Pennies might be in on it too. He might not be dead. Maybe he was acting. Didn't Robin Hood use a hollow reed to breathe underwater? What if the Pennies he saw was only a lifelike studio prop? In that case, what was he worried about? This was just entertainment.

That's what he wanted to believe. But the way Shelby Wills leaned across the table had left him cold.

Another train was on the way from the north. He hurried across the snow over the rails. Further off, he could see the train coming: a bright yellow headlight and a rumble. What were they carting around all day and night? Was America constantly being carved up and rearranged and moved from place to place?

The train blew its horn. If there was still a deer around it would have jumped into the nearest shadow. Or would it? The deer in town seemed to have adapted to the unnatural mechanical furnishings replacing their woods and creeks and meadows. They walked through it all like tourists from a more beautiful time.

Vatican understood. Sometimes he felt the same way.

The City Hall tower was dusted with snow. A web of black telephone line ran up the hill toward it. He followed Central Avenue. It could have been a road in the Roman Empire. Across to Prospect, it was a straight shot to the library. He felt for the book buried in his pocket. Every day the fine kept ticking. It was like carrying a time bomb.

He stopped beside a telephone pole and removed Issa's book. The due slip peeked from the top edge. That was how Shelby Wills tracked him down. He fanned through the pages until he came to the spot where his money was tipped in. He counted fourteen dollars. Suddenly he was rich! That was enough to pay his library fine and get some lunch afterwards. That made him hungry. He stuffed the bills in his coat and held on to the book. He was only a few blocks from the public library.

Vatican walked these streets every day but the snow made it feel like a different planet. He thought about a window seat in a warm café where he could spend the afternoon observing. That's what his mother did during the war. It was in his blood.

"Oh—" he rolled back on his heels, he still had to call her and tell her about the spoon. He looked to his right in The Leopold direction then his eyes wandered to the face staring at him from the telephone post like the animal on a totem pole. MISSING CAT. *If found or sighted please call.* There were other notices and signs stapled all over it—concerts, lost dogs, guitar lessons, cheap rental rooms and more. The telephone pole had a lot to say. Torn pages of conversation were left in fragments, some of them crisp as papyrus. A sky blue flyer with a picture of Martin's plane caught his eye.

YOU CAN FLY
OVER THE SEA!

Island Air Announces
Regular Passenger Service
by Air to Lemon Island
and Other Localities

Rates & Schedules
Beginning this Spring!

Vatican had to admit that was fast. Maybe Martin was right about bringing Shelby Wills on board. Finally his plane would soon be in the air.

He tried to picture it in place of where a crow shuffled overhead. The engine would sound like a lawnmower in the sky.

On the other side of the street, hopping on the snowy sidewalk in front of an apartment, a little kid squealed with excitement.

Vatican laughed. He wondered if they had school today. He remembered how that was; when the snow canceled school it felt like a holiday.

He had no reason to feel like a marked man. He wanted to feel like that kid instead.

A car parked by the curb overnight looked like it had been carved from a sugar cube. In the distance, between buildings, he caught a glimpse of the mountain.

A man on the corner of the next block was sowing salt on the sidewalk. Once Vatican got there he realized it wasn't salt, but some bright pink chemical. The man nodded at Vatican as they passed. Their feet didn't slip. The path to the library was scribbled with pink crayon.

Vatican watched his shoes and tried to use the footprints other people left behind. He thought about who would be following in what he left.

When she spoke, he gave a jump, but that was only half the surprise.

"Excuse me. Are you a registered voter?"

Vatican looked at the woman on the library steps and for a moment he couldn't breathe.

She wore a blue uniform with a patch sewn over

her heart. "I'm a volunteer with The Clean Air Action Group. Have you heard of our organization?"

He couldn't speak. Even a nod was too much.

She continued, "We're working to put on the ballot a measure to reduce the harmful emissions from that factory. Do you think clean water and air are important?"

He forced himself to say, "Yes," and as he did she smiled and The Shirelles began to sing.

"Would you like to add your name to our petition to show your support?"

He tried to look in her eyes for some sign this act wasn't real, while his voice repeated, "Yes."

She unsnapped a pen from the clipboard she held and passed it to him. He almost could have held her hand instead. It was the most difficult thing to only take the pen. It had to be her, but it couldn't be. She was long gone, wasn't she?

Vatican checked a box, printed his shaking name and the address for The Sea of Tranquility.

How could it be her? She was miles away from here and when she left she told him she would never be back. He tried to forget but he still remembered that rooftop and their song. He held out her clipboard and pen. Was it her or someone who looked just like her? Was that even possible? Was it that hard to believe?

She said, "We're having a meeting this Friday night at the community center at 7:30."

This time he tried to stay in her eyes. It was her. It had to be, but she wouldn't let on. She wouldn't break character. He said, "Okay," and she smiled—not the way you would for a lover, unless she was hiding that too.

It wasn't her. It had been so long, why would she

be doing this?

"Thank you," he said like a bird on a river.

"Thank *you*," she replied and that was her voice, wasn't it? Nobody else could sound like her. And the funny thing is, he knew this was something she would do. He knew her, didn't he?

"It will be nice to see you on Friday," she said. "We have things we can talk about."

Then, like someone catching fireflies, she moved quickly towards the next person nearing the library. "Excuse me, are you a registered voter?" just as if this was really her job and this was ordinary and they never had a song they would play for each other from the rooftop heights of this city long ago.

Look
Innocence is important
It has meaning
Look
It can give us
Hope against the very winds that we batter against it.

—Jack Spicer, from *Admonitions*

CHAPTER THIRTEEN

The #12

So how did Vatican Jones end up back at The Old Crown? Why would he return to the place that banished him to an alley? He was in a daze.

He found his table by the window. Some autopilot part of him carried him there. Steam on the glass formed tears that ran across the world outside. He didn't need the menu. The waitress asked if he wanted coffee and he said yes. When she asked him if he would like some food with that cup in front of him, he picked a number out of the air. "Okay," he said. "Can I have the twelfth thing on the menu?" He had no idea what that was going to be.

She knew. That was part of her job to know. From the look in her eyes, he wondered if he just ordered a bowl of coal. "The #12," she hesitantly said. From the sound of her voice, he guessed she might have to go to the basement to fill a pail from the chute of piled charcoal. She would hand it to the cook who would sear the black edges in a pan—a meal for an iron-lined stomach, like the boiler of a steamship a mile out at sea.

Vatican sipped his coffee and stared past the factory. The bay looked like a chalkboard…white luffs of waves kicked up by the wind running between the islands. He thought of what happened on the library steps. Time should have taken her too but she was right back again.

He had half a cup of coffee in his hands.

"VJ, I heard about what happened yesterday." It was the waitress who liked him. "I'm sorry." He knew she always said hello and goodbye to him and smiled whenever she did. She slid her hand in her apron pocket and showed five dollars. "Do you need money for your coffee today?"

Vatican tapped the library book lying flat beside his napkin. "I found my wallet, thanks anyway."

After she topped his coffee, before she returned to the kitchen, she said, "I heard you ordered #12." He never saw her stare at him that way before. He couldn't find an answer because he didn't know what he had done. He settled for a shrug. Whatever happened was on the way. The wheels were in motion. There was no stopping it now. She knew there was something wrong, he could see it in her eyes, but she was headed out of the way, carrying her Sylex back to the kitchen.

Vatican took his hand off Issa's book. He realized he walked right past the library's book drop and forgot to return it. Who wouldn't forget? He had just seen a ghost.

Cupped around the coffee, his hands drank in the heat and he let it radiate up his arms, all the way down to his cold feet.

Dark clouds bunched over the island. He imagined there was a factory up in those clouds and cogwheels were spinning, the assembly line was filling…in another hour or so it would start to snow. That was okay, he wasn't far from home. The Sea of Tranquility was just across the street.

He let go of his cup and covered his hot hands over his face. With his eyes shut he realized what was missing from the room. No music…only the ordinary ambiance of a café. It could be a dull new record in a jukebox where Pennies used to be.

The song didn't last long. It was interrupted by the

clop, clop footsteps headed his way. There were at least three different waitresses who worked The Old Crown and this was his nemesis. She wore wooden clogs that sounded like a horse on a diving board. Usually they avoided each other, but not this time. Like the alligator in Peter Pan, he knew she was coming.

"Do you have money today?" She crossed her arms and glared.

"Yes," Vatican said, "in my book." He reached for his haiku wallet and picked it up. He fanned the pages but it was only filled with poems and the overdue receipt.

For a moment panic turned him ice cold.

Then he remembered he moved the money to his pocket. What a relief that fourteen dollars felt as he flattened the crumpled bills on top of Issa's book.

She said, "You're lucky today."

Yes, he thought, I am.

She stomped past another table, past someone holding a hand in the air with an empty cup needing a refill.

Vatican had to count this as a victory. Why shouldn't he stop here for a feast? You never knew when it would be your last. He was living in the present with his $14.

But the past wasn't done with him yet. He was about to be served the #12. The chef rang the bell and the waitress took the shallow tureen. It was heavy. She needed both hands to carry it. She didn't want to spill the deep red broth. Every step across the floor had to be planned carefully, relayed by radar. She held it higher as a little girl ran underneath chasing a ball. Had anyone ever ordered this dish before? She only heard stories.

All the way to the window without spilling a drop,

she set it down on the table and rubbed the burn in her arms. It figured he would be the one to order the #12. He had the look of a lighthouse keeper who had seen a steamship drown. "Here you are," she said. Her work was done. She could fly back to the kitchen. She couldn't watch that red glow burning like Dresden anymore.

Vatican looked at it and looked away. Where was Pennies' music? The room had gone quiet except for the dull thudding beat of a baked heart.

He wanted to believe that was tomato soup it swam in. He wanted to believe it wasn't ever so slightly breathing, living, pumping blood and singing so quietly only he could hear. He listened and the glistening sight soon had him hypnotized.

Vatican followed it, falling weightless, down deep. He went back to where he first met her, on a different street in a different city long ago. He returned to a sidewalk on a rainy night. Yes, one of those classic rainy Seattle nights when the leaves shine with pearls, the wet streets hiss and the smell of earth rises from cement. Not a hard rain, just light. The Neptune Theatre was around the corner, the steep blue roof of IHOP, the back of Tower Records across the parking lot. Cars were parked bumper to bumper beside the curb, wet as seals. A row of Japanese maple trees was planted like umbrellas. Vatican was walking along Brooklyn Avenue and she called his name.

He saw a dark haired girl on the steps of an old brick apartment building. He didn't know how she knew who he was. They must have met somewhere before.

"Can you help me move something to my car?"'

In those days he didn't have much to do or anywhere

to go. There was a tide in Seattle as sure as the one that washed around Puget Sound. It rose over the banks of Alaskan Way, up Pike and Pine and Union and rode in the air everywhere. He learned to ride with it. And he knew she was part of the pull. How else could he explain it? He was carried to her by an invisible force. The current that brought them together poured them into a red carpeted hall, to an opened apartment door. The lights were on and emptiness filled the floor except for a pyramid of boxes. A fishbowl on top of a stereo with a red goldfish who swam round and round.

The tide he let carry him to sights all over the city took him over to the bird pattern wallpaper and the big wooden keyboard cabinet docked like a barge. It looked heavy. No wonder she needed help moving it. She took one end and he took the other. In a few years he would be used to a wooden box not much bigger than this.

She said, "Have you ever seen an Optigan before?"

"Is that what this is?"

She nodded. She had to twist so they could tip it through the doorway.

Everything was just like it was happening again. The baked heart read his mind and put him there.

"What does an Optigan do?" he winced. It was heavy enough to hold a rhinoceros. Now they were going down the steps. There were only three fortunately.

She told him about the Optigan as they pushed it along the path to the sidewalk. The rain felt good. The wheels clattered and caught in the cement cracks.

"Where's your car?"

"Right there," she said. "That's George."

George was a moon colored Volkswagen Beetle.

The rain made the car shine like an egg. Vatican hoped the Optigan had a button to turn it into a suitcase. How else was it going to fit inside that little car?

But she opened the door and pulled the seats forward and she went in backwards carrying one end while he lifted and pushed the Optigan from the curb. If only a circus ringmaster happened to be passing by. They would have been made into stars overnight.

One of the best ways to get to know someone is taking on what seems like an impossible task. She laughed at the way he muttered and wheezed like W.C. Fields and her laugh was like Optigan music to his ears.

"See!" she said at last. "We did it!"

"This door won't close," he said, pushing on it.

"That's okay. You can hold it while we drive."

"Where are we going?"

"The movie theater," she said. "That's where I work. We can store it in the basement. Hop in!"

It's easy to forget there is a heart underneath everything happening. That night his was beating like crazy. He didn't know if Seattle still had that kind of rain. He didn't go there now. It was 1992. A lot had changed.

The car's slanted seats pushed forward by the Optigan held them both pressed to the windshield glass.

"I have to move out of my apartment tonight," she told him. "I can keep the rest of my stuff in my car. It's just for a couple days until my new apartment opens up."

He knew the feeling; once he had to do that. He found a better place and he was trying to skip rent but the manager caught him carrying his mattress out the door.

Driving this way with her was like sitting in the front row at the movies. They were almost falling into the rainy picture show. Everything had a dew-like quality though it wasn't morning. He kept hearing her laugh.

They found a parking spot on East Roy, just across from The Harvard Exit and she thanked Saint Frances. "She's the patron saint of parking," she explained. "There's a saint for everything."

"Alright," he said, trying out a cramped bow, "thanks Saint Frances. Now, do you have a saint to get me out of the car? Is there a patron saint of shoehorns?"

She laughed. It was still raining but they were parked under a big tree full of black leaves. The theater was across the street. The Optigan didn't have far to go.

He remembered how they brought it down the alley. Ivy grew up along the brick wall. She had a key for the carriage door. An ancient latch used to open to horses back when people rode them through the streets. Some boxes were already stored beneath the cobwebs. They wheeled the Optigan over there and left it. It looked like Count Dracula's coffin. That was the last they saw of it. The next time she looked, it would be gone.

But they didn't know that then.

They went upstairs into the lobby. The light fixtures resembled candles. White drapes covered the windows. A table held a big silver urn full of hot tea. Every time he had orange spice, he thought of that place. The sound of a movie played through the wall. She poured a cup of tea for each of them. That first sip warmed him. Vatican didn't know a heart was causing this. It was still the 1980s and he had time before he would know.

CHAPTER FOURTEEN

The Sea of Tranquility

Across the street on the corner, Cinema Books glowed. Car headlights slowed. Vatican was starting to feel like this was only a dream that could change at any moment, but it wasn't over yet. They stopped beside her car and she asked, "Can I drive you somewhere, wherever you were going before I borrowed you?"

"I don't know. I was just wandering." He could easily follow Aloha to 24th Ave, walk downhill and cross the Mountlake Bridge back into the University District. It would only be an hour drifting with the tide.

"Come on," she said, putting her hand on his. "I'll take you somewhere."

It was nice to get back in her car. It was their chariot. It would take them out of Seattle one day and it would be the car he was in whenever he dreamed.

When they pushed the seats back, he found a red Cellophane Square record store bag at his feet.

She said, "Oh, those are for the Optigan."

"It plays records too?" He rubbed his sore shoulder, "Too bad it never learned to walk."

She laughed, "Those are the disks I told you about. They go in the Optigan and you can play along with them. Take a look." She swung the steering wheel. They were already on Aloha. Raindrops made dots run on the glass.

Vatican lifted the stack free of the bag and read the first title, "Latin Fever." He pulled that disk partially from its sleeve. It was clear as glass. He could see the rainy city through it. He could see her on the other side. Was the car radio on? Did she do that? He heard a deep underwater drum. KCMU played ethereal music sometimes, maybe that's what it was. He slid that ghost of a record back in its sleeve and read the next ones to her. "Big Band Beat, Bluegrass Banjo, Polynesian Village…" It sounded like a shipwrecked radio in the car. "Country Waltz, Rollin' Easy..." All this happened long ago and it was hard to hold. The titles were fading in and out. "Romantic Strings…" Weight and substance were like clutching something in a dream. Vatican was slipping away, the spell was wearing off. "The Blues Sweet and Low." The beat of the drum was slowing, stopping. It was gone.

Vatican was back in 1992.

He sat at the table in The Old Crown Café the same as before but the #12 wasn't there.

Nickels was finishing a song. He sat where Pennies sat yesterday. "This next number is one I learned from a Johnny Cash cassette. Unfortunately, the tape cut off halfway through the song. I don't know how it ends. But I'll play you what I know. This is called 'Don't Forget to Give My Love to Rose' or half of it or so."

Vatican knew it was time to go. He left his money where it was, took his book and began to stand. The ceiling bent as he got to his feet. He would have to be careful. The tables tipped like flowers and people were busy as bees around them. He took a step then another and had to imagine he was one of those freight trains rushing through town. All he heard was the wind. He knocked a copy of *The Wise Penny* off the rack by the door but he wasn't going to stop. There was no time for that. He had to get out.

He was surprised to see snow. The last place he had been, a daydream screened by a baked beating heart, was a dark city in the rain.

Then he almost ran right into 99. She was in the middle of the sidewalk with her bag of flyers, staring up the hill, knowing she had a long day ahead of her, standing in front of the record store, or the photocopy shop, on the coldest feet in town.

"Oh!" he said. "Sorry!"

As her attention turned to him, he could see the wheels start to spin. The words she used for everyone were about to ramble out. He stopped them before they could start. He didn't need another flyer, not even to start a fire with.

Vatican said, "Do you know who that is getting signatures at the library?"

It looked like he had broken her. The factory in her mind that made the same words like cars on an assembly line had been sabotaged. Her eyes were hubcaps he could see himself in.

"Sorry," he said again. "I just thought you might know." And he left her alone, staring into the desolate space that was empty without her speech driving round and round. She would have to start all over from the very beginning, with the invention of the wheel. At a blackboard in a little one-room schoolhouse with tumbleweeds for a playground, she would hold a broken bone of chalk and write: *Everything in the store is 99 cents* over and over until her mantra covered the walls.

A bus with chains clanked up Holly. It sounded angry and medieval. The windows showed only fog. Vatican waited for a blue station wagon before he made his way across. Loud radio trailed behind it.

One patch of ice shined in the middle of the road like the back of a whale breaking through. He was careful putting his feet on that.

A thick cloud surrounded the factory. He thought of 99 and looked back. He didn't want her to be stuck to the cement like a statue. It was okay though, she was already somewhere else. He was sure her words were working again, handing out flyers with mittens.

As he passed Sinbad's, he couldn't resist looking in the window. The display was always changing slightly. Something new would appear in something else's place. He felt entranced but didn't want anything more. He still carried the spoon he didn't know what to do with.

A cardboard box on a checkered table cloth. A Revell model kit—not a P-38 warplane or the PT-109—the lid was a painting of his wooden houseboat floating at sea. The bright lettering read: *Balsa HAIKU. Easy to Make!* Seagulls wheeled around it. The wind filled its square orange sail. Vatican couldn't tell if that was him holding the lines. Other words printed in red said: *As Seen on TV!* He was glad he didn't have any money. He might have gone inside to buy it.

Anyway, it was too cold to contemplate and he had already been through enough. The Sea of Tranquility was around the corner—that's where he could catch his breath.

Someone had shoveled the crust of snow off the sidewalk in front of the antique store. He imagined it was done by one of those dramatic Norman Rockwell kids who had been pushed out of a painting frame, bundled up with a long red knit scarf while a mother and a cat watched from a kitchen window.

The scream of a train down in the cold yard surprised him. It sounded like the shriek from a slaughterhouse. He thought of *Murder Conductor* and that model kit. He wondered how they already knew about Haiku before they filmed. They must have sent scouts ahead of the show to study the town. They found The Sea of Tranquility and they knew the story before they arrived. Across America, how many model kits were sold and how many Haiku were being built?

Or, what if that kit in the window was the only one? What if it was just another prop for the TV camera sweeping along? Vatican wasn't sure about anything, only looking forward to being home.

The snow in the narrow driveway was disturbed by thick tire tracks. The treads made the ground look like alligator skin. A lot of footprints trampled it too. For a moment Vatican was hopeful that a truck had brought Haiku back. That would be nice to open the door and see it returned to the spot where it belonged. Maybe things could go back to normal.

As soon as he unlocked the door and went in, he knew that wouldn't be true.

The room was empty. No Haiku. No airplane. What was happening?

"Martin?"

No answer.

Vatican was an echo walking across the wooden floor. Only his cot remained, waiting for orders to charge into the next nightmare.

He called, "Martin?" once more but it was no use. Martin and his seaplane had been hauled off in a truck. Another couple hours of snow and those tracks in the driveway would disappear too. The Sea of Tranquility had become like its namesake on the moon.

Vatican wondered what he was supposed to do.

He didn't have long to wonder.

The door onto Holly opened and there was his

answer.

Shelby Wills entered and shut the door. The gust of wind she also let in spun itself in a cold circle then settled down. If he could have seen it, he supposed it would resemble a Great Dane, huffing and puffing chilly breath on the floor. Shelby Wills approached Vatican slowly. She had all the time in the world.

Vatican had a feeling he did not.

What was she going to do, pull a gun on him? Could his Issa book stop a bullet?

"My poor unfortunate friend," she said. "Looks like you don't have anything anymore." She had cornered him and she knew it. She was close enough to hold him down with a claw. But her voice purred again, "We don't often have two murders on our show. One is usually enough, wouldn't you say? Well…" she drew a breath and let it out as a cold cloud, "Not this time."

Vatican's voice was dry. "You're supposed to be a crime solver, not a murderer."

With an unwarm smile, she asked, "Is that so? And do you believe everything you see on the TV, Mr. Jones? Hmmm?"

He didn't know if he should run. He didn't know where he would run to…Anywhere far away.

She let him stand there, petrified, as she regarded the empty workshop. "On the other hand, your friend Martin is doing quite well. We moved the airplane and him to a far more filmable location—a lovely old cedar lodge in the trees, on the quiet water of a lake where there aren't any trains or cars or beggars in the street. You should see the place! At the end of the program we'll let Martin take off in his plane, with that view of the mountain all snowy in the distance." She smiled but her eyes were hard and cold as stones.

"I wonder if I should let you see that place. Would you like that? A little borrowed time, Mr. Jones?"

He nodded. It was all he could do.

"Oh," she paused, "before I go…" She reached into her coat pocket. He didn't suppose it would be a gun, not if she meant to show him that beautiful place on the lake. She held out her hand, "Can you hold onto this for me in the meantime?" He didn't have to look at his palm to know the feel of that hot black coin. "Don't lose it this time, hmmm?"

CHAPTER FIFTEEN

Evening, 1992

Vatican was living on borrowed time. He knew it too. He felt the pages running out.

Out on Holly Street it was cold. It was getting dark already and more snow telegraphed in the air as he walked the three blocks to The Leopold. His hands were thrust in pockets and he still had that library book tucked under his arm. Issa had been a companion this whole adventure, he might as well stay until the end.

Vatican didn't know how Shelby Wills would make that happen. A bullet? Poison? Would she drop an anvil on him from a roof? With that black coin in his pocket it wouldn't be long.

He didn't want to give it to someone again and he doubted he could throw it off the edge of a dock. He had a feeling it would float right back to him somehow. Shelby Wills would know…Or was her bloodhound tracking that coin? Pennies didn't even survive a night. Was that old dog her instrument of death?

Vatican breathed the cold air. If he died now, he would miss spring. Then he would miss summer. Fall and winter were good too. But who would believe his story that the star of *Murder Conductor* was actually the one doing the killing? Over all these years along the rail lines of America, the bodies were piling up. And now he was about to become one too. Why would the police believe his story? Shelby Wills was one of them.

If you lived inside a box on a factory floor by the railroad tracks, you got used to the sounds of the city, all the motors in the air. When there was snow, all those sounds were muffled and tamped. It was like walking on the moon.

Did anyone ever get away from Shelby Wills? He had to have faith that he could. After all, he already escaped once. It was in the script that he was meant to die and he passed the coin off. Couldn't he do it again somehow? He thought about that as he walked by the Woolworths' windows. The old Avalon used to be next door. He remembered seeing *Radar Men from the Moon* there. Movies and TV shows like that inspired the creation of Vatican Jones. He became a hero who could battle any kind of evil, solve any crime and travel through time. Why couldn't he employ those skills to get out of his predicament? Shelby Wills couldn't always win.

Cornwall led to The Leopold. It was a retirement home now, a nine story tower of memories. He remembered when it was a hotel and John Wayne stayed there. Tonight it looked gloomy as a castle.

A yellow taxi splashed in the street. Vatican cut across its wake. He had to hop over a puddle with ice in it. His feet were just as wet and cold as a frogman.

Would he be making his last stand at The Leopold? There was no way he could know.

The golden lights of the Crystal Ballroom spilled out the windows and made ponds on the sidewalk. Vatican waded into the first pool and looked inside. A couple were having soup next to the glass. He took note they were eating tomato soup. There were plenty of tables in the dining room. He could choose one against the wall with a good view of the door. Or he could take the stairs.

Nobody seemed to mind him wandering off the street, stopping in to use the telephone in the basement. He never caught anyone's attention at the reception desk, he went right to the stairway as usual.

One of Martin's friends told Vatican about the phone booth in the basement. It was after Vatican's mother died and Vatican was being dragged around by a shadow. "Go to The Leopold," Martin's friend told him. "You can talk to her again." His eyes shined like a circus fortune teller.

Vatican never questioned it. Why would he? If something so magical could exist in the world, it was a miracle.

It was a miracle that had to be kept hidden at the end of a hallway underground. Vatican tried to visit once a week. Sometimes he forgot. Then the next time he called she would sound further away. He had to coax her voice back from a cloud.

Not many people used these steps. Halfway down sat a green can of Comet that might have been left there in 1983. Vatican noticed it every time. It was solemn as a park statue.

Instead of lampposts with their lights up in the leafy stars and halos of moths, the hall was like the lower deck of a trawler. He half expected to see a stowaway hiding behind a stack of boxes.

The hall ended with a wooden phone booth pushed against the concrete wall. There used to be a booth like that in the old train station. He thought they had all disappeared like the buffalo.

This one looked as if it had been handcrafted at a shop that also carved cuckoo clocks. His reflection grew in the glass portions of the door. He was glad it wasn't the ghost of the ancient mariner staring back at him.

Just as Martin's friend told him to, Vatican

stepped inside. Once in that wooden box, he felt the drastic change in temperature. Like a beehive, the air molecules hummed and rubbed. Vatican closed the squeaking door and sat on the bench. It was silent as a tomb. He set Issa next to him. There was just enough room. He took the phone receiver off its cradle and brought it to his ear.

What would it sound like to hear the wind from another world? The phone had nothing to say.

He needed money to make it work.

Did he have any money?

He left it all at The Old Crown, didn't he? He pictured the spot on the tabletop where the #12 had been. His pockets were empty, weren't they?

Not quite.

He had one coin to his name.

He had to give it some thought though…It seemed like the perfect fate for that haunted coin. It belonged to death. So go ahead, let her bloodhound track it to this basement phone booth. Nobody on the line could be hurt, they were already dead.

After he dropped that coal of a coin into the slot, the phone worked fine.

He told the operator he wanted to speak with his mother.

"One moment please while I put through your call."

"Thank you," he said.

In between the times they talked, he wondered where his mother was. It seemed like someone always had to go looking for her, as if she was a bit of cloud that had to be shepherded back. He should have asked her. Wouldn't that be nice to know what to expect when you leave this life? For some reason he never thought to ask when he had her on the phone. Honestly, what did it matter as long as she sounded happy where she was? That was enough.

As soon as he heard her hello, he chimed in, "Hi mom, it's me. Victory."

There wasn't a lot to say—he didn't want to worry her about murder—and before he knew it, he was telling her about the weather. "It snowed today."

That seemed pretty interesting to her, but then he remembered, "Oh, let me tell you the reason I called. You know that antique store? I found a spoon from The Old Sea Gull for sale...Yes, I bought it...Not much, a few dollars. Do you think it's the same one you borrowed? Do you know what happened to that one?"

She said she wasn't sure. She said that happened so long ago and it didn't matter really; everything had a way of working out.

"But what should I do with it? I wanted to return it but The Old Sea Gull is long gone. There's a bank there now...I know...I know...I just wanted to—"

The operator interrupted, "Please deposit another twenty five cents."

The haunted coin didn't last as long as he hoped it would.

"That's all the time I have for now. I have to let you go...Okay, you too. See you soon."

Vatican thought about that after he hung up. Would he see her soon?

Only if Shelby Wills caught him...Then he would find himself in that telephone-land where a cloud taxi would take him to meet all the people he missed and this town would mean nothing in a little while.

Vatican stepped free of the booth. The hall and the

122

stairs and the lobby of The Leopold bid him goodbye.

Outside, he was in the cold night tide. He could feel it going back to sea, strong enough to take anything that wasn't barnacled down. A wind creature pushed him too. They seemed to be having a fine time this evening, surfing in front of the snow.

The sidewalk slid towards the bay, to the last street and the railroad track. The trains were always coming and going, slipping out of town. He could find the open door of a boxcar—there was bound to be one the inspector forgot to check on his clipboard—and he could crawl in there and find a big shadow to hide in. Once that train gave a jolt and started to move, it would pick up speed. The click of the wheels going faster, the rush of the wind and flashes of city lights. The horn would tell the world that Vatican Jones was leaving. Then he remembered who was waiting for him Friday night—"We have things we can talk about"—and he would lean out the door to see if there was still time to jump off.

ISLAND AIR
written by Allen Frost
September 2018-June 2019

Books by Good Deed Rain

Saint Lemonade, Allen Frost, 2014. Two novels illustrated by the author in the manner of the old Big Little Books.

Playground, Allen Frost, 2014. Poems collected from seven years of chapbooks.

Roosevelt, Allen Frost, 2015. A Pacific Northwest novel set in July, 1942, when a boy and a girl search for a missing elephant. Illustrated throughout by Fred Sodt.

5 Novels, Allen Frost, 2015. Novels written over five years, featuring circus giants, clockwork animals, detectives and time travelers.

The Sylvan Moore Show, Allen Frost, 2015. A short story omnibus of 193 stories written over 30 years.

Town in a Cloud, Allen Frost, 2015. A 3-part book of poetry, written during the Bellingham rainy seasons of fall, winter, and spring.

A Flutter of Birds Passing Through Heaven: A Tribute to Robert Sund. 2016. Edited by Allen Frost and Paul Piper. The story of a legendary Ish River poet & artist.

At the Edge of America, Allen Frost, 2016. Two novels in one book blend time travel in a mythical poetic America.

Lake Erie Submarine, Allen Frost, 2016. A two week vacation in Ohio inspired these poems, illustrated by the author.

and Light, Paul Piper, 2016. Poetry written over three years. Illustrated with watercolors by Penny Piper.

The Book of Ticks, Allen Frost, 2017. A giant collection of 8 mysterious adventures featuring Phil Ticks. Illustrated throughout by Aaron Gunderson.

I Can Only Imagine, Allen Frost, 2017. Five adventures of love and heartbreak dreamed in an imaginary world. Cover & color illustrations by Annabelle Barrett.

The Orphanage of Abandoned Teenagers, Allen Frost, 2017. A fictional guide for teens and their parents. Illustrated by the author.

In the Valley of Mystic Light: An Oral History of the Skagit Valley Arts Scene, 2017. Edited by Claire Swedberg & Rita Hupy.

Different Planet, Allen Frost, 2017. Four science fiction adventures: reincarnation, robots, talking animals, outer space and clones. Cover & illustrations by Laura Vasyutynska.

Go with the Flow: A Tribute to Clyde Sanborn. 2018. Edited by Allen Frost. The life and art of a timeless river poet.

Homeless Sutra, Allen Frost, 2018. Four stories: Sylvan Moore, a flying monk, a water salesman, and a guardian rabbit.

The Lake Walker, Allen Frost 2018. A little novel set in black and white like one of those old European movies about death and life.

A Hundred Dreams Ago, Allen Frost, 2018. A winter book of poetry and prose. Illustrated by Aaron Gunderson.

Almost Animals, Allen Frost, 2018. A collection of linked stories, thinking about what makes us animals.

The Robotic Age, Allen Frost, 2018. A vaudeville magician and his faithful robot track down ghosts. Illustrated throughout by Aaron Gunderson.

Kennedy, Allen Frost, 2018. This sequel to *Roosevelt* is a coming-of-age fable set during two weeks in 1962 in a mythical Kennedy-land. Illustrated throughout by Fred Sodt.

Fable, Allen Frost, 2018. There's something going on in this country and I can best relate it in fable: the parable of the rabbits, a bedtime story, and the diary of our trip to Ohio.

Elbows & Knees: Essays & Plays, Allen Frost, 2018. A thrilling collection of writing about some of my favorite subjects, from B-movies to Brautigan.

The Last Paper Stars, Allen Frost 2019. A trip back in time to the 20 year old mind of Frankenstein, and two other worlds of the future.

Walt Amherst is Awake, Allen Frost, 2019. The dreamlife of an office worker. Illustrated throughout by Aaron Gunderson.

When You Smile You Let in Light, Allen Frost, 2019. An atomic love story written by a 23 year old.

Pinocchio in America, Allen Frost, 2019. After 82 years buried underground, Pinocciton returns to life behind a car repair shop in America.

Taking Her Sides on Immortality, Robert Huff, 2019. The long awaited poetry colleciton from a local, nationally renowned master of words.

Florida, Allen Frost, 2019. Three days in Florida turned into a book of sunshine inspired stories.

Blue Anthem Wailing, Allen Frost, 2019. My first novel written in college is an apocalyptic, Old Testament race through American shadows while Amelia Earhart flies overhead.

The Welfare Office, Allen Frost, 2019. The animals go in and out of the office, leaving these stories as footprints.

Island Air, Allen Frost, 2019. A detective novel featuring haiku, a lost library book and streetsongs.

DATE DUE

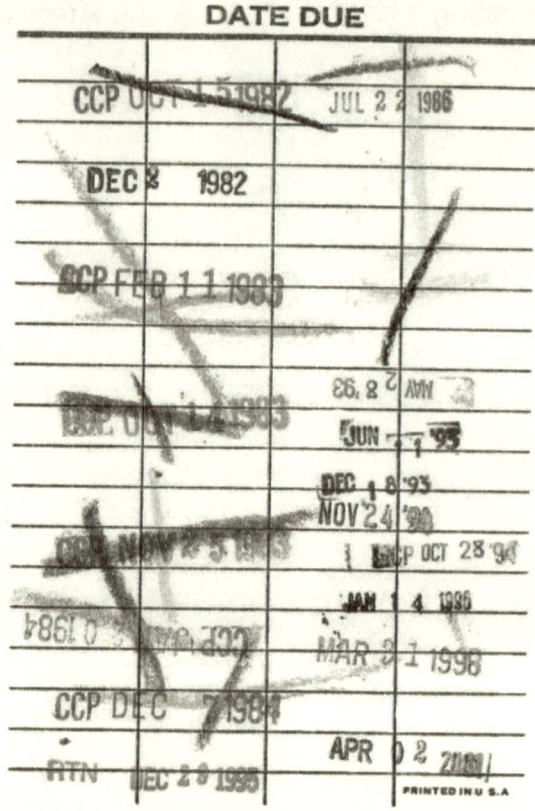

132

www.ingramcontent.com/pod-product-compliance
Lightning Source LLC
Chambersburg PA
CBHW050150110726
47898CB00008B/2749